# teen IDOL

# MEG CABOT

HARPERCOLLINS*PUBLISHERS*

Teen Idol
Copyright © 2004 by Meggin Cabot
All rights reserved. No part of this book may be used or repro-
duced in any manner whatsoever without written permission
except in the case of brief quotations embodied in critical arti-
cles and reviews. Printed in the United States of America. For
information address HarperCollins Children's Books, a division
of HarperCollins Publishers, 1350 Avenue of the Americas,
New York, NY 10019.
www.harperchildrens.com

Library of Congress Cataloging-in-Publication Data
Cabot, Meg.
    Teen idol / Meg Cabot. —1st ed.
      p.   cm.
    Summary: When teenage heartthrob Luke Striker shows up
at a small-town Indiana high school to do research for a movie
role, he persuades junior Jenny Greenley to use her consider-
able talents to try to change things at school for the better.
    ISBN 0-06-009616-0
    ISBN 0-06-009617-9 (library binding)
    [1. High schools—Fiction.    2. Schools—Fiction.
3.Interpersonal relations—Fiction.    4. Conduct of life—
Fiction.    5. Actors and actresses—Fiction.    6. Indiana—
Fiction.]    I. Title.
PZ7+                                              2003024203
[Fic]—dc22

Typography by Sasha Illingworth
1   2   3   4   5   6   7   8   9   10
❖
First Edition

*To Benjamin*

## Acknowledgments

Many thanks to all of those who helped in the creation of this book, including Beth Ader, Jennifer Brown, Bill Contardi, Michele Jaffe, Laura Langlie, and Abigail McAden, and the faculty and students of Bloomington High School South, circa 1981–1985, on whom the author swears none of the characters in this book are based.

# Ask Annie

**Ask Annie your most complex interpersonal relationship questions. Go on, we dare you! All letters to Annie are subject to publication in the Clayton High School *Register*. Names and e-mail addresses of correspondents guaranteed confidential.**

Dear Annie,

My stepmom keeps telling me that everything I like is evil, and that I shouldn't like this or that because when I die I will go to hell. She thinks liking rock music, reading fantasy books, and watching MTV is sinful. She goes on and on about how the music, books, and people I like are all evil.

I respect what she likes, and I think she should respect what I like, too. What do you think, Annie?

Going to Hell

Dear Going to Hell,

Tell your stepmom to cool it. You aren't going to hell. You're already in it.

It's called high school.

Annie

*One*

*I witnessed the* kidnapping of Betty Ann Mulvaney.

Well, me and the twenty-three other people in first period Latin class at Clayton High School (student population 1,200).

Unlike everybody else, however, I actually did something to try to stop it. Well, sort of. I went, "Kurt. What are you doing?"

Kurt just rolled his eyes. He was all, "Relax, Jen. It's a joke, okay?"

But, see, there really isn't anything all that funny in the way Kurt Schraeder swiped Betty Ann from Mrs. Mulvaney's desk, then stuffed her into his JanSport. Some of her yellow yarn hair got caught in the teeth of his backpack's zipper and everything.

Kurt didn't care. He just went right on zipping.

I should have said something more. I should have said, *Put her back, Kurt.*

Only I didn't. I didn't because . . . well, I'll get back to that part later. Besides, I knew it was a lost cause. Kurt was already high-fiving all of his friends, the other jocks who hang in the back row and are only taking the class (for the second time, having already taken it their junior year and apparently not having done so well) in hopes of getting higher scores on the verbal part of the SATs, not out of any love for Latin culture or because they heard Mrs. Mulvaney is a good teacher or whatever.

Kurt and his buds had to hide their smirks behind their *Paulus et Lucia* workbooks when Mrs. Mulvaney came in after the second bell, a steaming cup of coffee in her hand.

As she does every morning, Mrs. Mulvaney sang, *"Aurora interea miseris mortalibus almam extulerat lucem referens opera atque labores,"* to us (basically: "It's another sucky morning, now let's get to work"), then picked up a piece of chalk and commanded us to write out the present tense of *gaudeo, -ere*.

She didn't even notice Betty Ann was gone.

Not until third period, anyway, when my best friend Trina—short for Catrina: she says she doesn't think of herself as particularly feline, only, you know, I'm not so sure I agree—who has her for class then, says that Mrs. Mulvaney was in the middle of explaining the past participle when she noticed the empty spot on her desk.

According to Trina, Mrs. Mulvaney went, "Betty Ann?" in this funny high-pitched voice.

By then of course the entire school knew that Kurt Schraeder had Betty Ann stuffed in his locker. Still, nobody said anything. That's because everybody likes Kurt.

Well, that isn't true, exactly. But the people who don't like Kurt are too afraid to say anything, because Kurt is president of the senior class and captain of the football team and could crush them with a glance, like Magneto from *X-Men*.

Not really, of course, but you get my drift. I mean, you don't cross a guy like Kurt Schraeder. If he wants to kidnap a teacher's Cabbage Patch doll, you just let him, because otherwise you'll end up eating your lunch all by yourself out by the flagpole like Cara Cow or run the risk of having Tater Tots hurled at your head or whatever.

The thing is, though, Mrs. Mulvaney loves that stupid doll. I mean, every year on the first day of school, she dresses it up in this stupid Clayton High cheerleader outfit she had made at So-Fro Fabrics.

And on Halloween, she puts Betty Ann in this little witch suit, with a pointed hat and a tiny broom and everything. Then at Christmas she dresses Betty Ann like an elf. There's an Easter outfit, too, though Mrs. Mulvaney doesn't call it that, because of the whole separation-of-church-and-state thing. Mrs. Mulvaney just calls it Betty Ann's spring dress.

But it totally comes with this little flowered bonnet and a basket filled with real robin's eggs that somebody gave her a long time ago, probably back in the eighties, which was when some ancient graduating class presented Mrs. Mulvaney with Betty Ann in the first place. On account of them feeling sorry for Mrs. Mulvaney, since she's a really, really good teacher, but she has never been able to have any kids of her own.

Or so the story goes. I don't know if it's true or not. Well, except for the part about Mrs. M. being a good teacher. Because she totally is. And the part about her not having any kids of her own.

But the rest of it . . . I don't know.

What I do know is, here it is, almost the last month of my junior year—Betty Ann had been wearing her summer outfit, a pair of overalls with a straw hat, like Huck Finn, when she disappeared—and I was sitting around worrying about her. A doll. A stupid *doll*.

"You don't think they're going to do anything to her, do you?" I asked Trina later that same day, during show choir. Trina worries that I don't have enough extracurriculars on my transcript, since all I like to do is read. So she suggested I take show choir with her.

Except that it turns out that Trina *slightly* misrepresented what show choir is all about. Instead of just a fun extra-curricular, it's turned out to be this huge deal—I had to audition and everything. I'm not the world's best singer or anything, but they really needed altos, and since I guess I'm an alto, I got in. Altos mostly just go la-la-la on the same note while the sopranos sing all these scales and words and stuff, so it's cool, because basically I can just sit there and go la-la-la on the same note and read a book since Karen Sue Walters, the soprano who sits on the riser in front of me, has totally huge hair, and Mr. Hall, the director of the Troubadours—that's right: our school choir even has its own name—can't see what I'm doing.

Mr. Hall does make all the girls wear padded bras under our blouses for "uniformity of appearance" while we perform, which is kind of bogus, but whatever. It looks good on your transcript. Being in show choir. Not the bras.

The thing I'm not sure I'll ever forgive Trina for is the dancing. Seriously. We have to dance as we sing . . . well, not dance, really, but like move our arms. And I'm not the world's best arm mover. I have no sense of rhythm whatso-ever . . .

Something Mr. Hall feels compelled to point out about three times a day.

"What if they cut off her ear?" I whispered to Trina. I had to whisper, because Mr. Hall was working with the tenors a few risers away. We are preparing for this very big statewide show choir competition—Bishop Luers, it's called—and Mr. Hall's been way tense about it. Like, he's been yelling at me about my arm movements four or even *five* times a day, instead of just the normal three. "And they send it to Mrs. M. with a ransom note? They won't do anything like that, will they, do you think? I mean, that's destruction of personal property."

"Oh my God," Trina said. She's a first soprano and sits next to Karen Sue Walters. First sopranos, I've noticed, are kind of bossy. But I guess it's sort of understandable, since they also have to do all the work, you know, hitting those high notes. "Would you get a grip? It's just a prank, okay? The seniors pull one every year. What is with you, anyway? You weren't this upset over the stupid goat."

Last year's graduating class's prank was putting a goat on the roof of the gym. I don't even know what's supposed to be funny about this. I mean, the goat could have been seriously injured.

"It's just . . ." I couldn't get the picture of Betty Ann's yarn hair getting caught in that zipper out of my head. "It just seems so *wrong*. Mrs. Mulvaney really loves that doll."

"Whatever," Trina said. "It's just a doll."

Except to Mrs. Mulvaney, Betty Ann is more than just a doll. I'm pretty sure.

Anyway, the whole thing was bugging me so much that after school, when I got to the offices of the *Register*—that's the school paper where I work most days . . . not to build up my extracurriculars, but because I actually kind of like it—I blurted out at the staff meeting that somebody ought to do a story on it. The kidnapping of Betty Ann Mulvaney, I mean.

"A story," Geri Lynn Packard said. "On a doll."

Geri Lynn jiggled her can of Diet Coke as she spoke. Geri Lynn likes her Diet Coke flat, so she jiggles the can until it gets that way before she drinks from it. I personally find a taste for flat soda a little weird, but that isn't actually the weirdest thing about Geri Lynn. The weirdest thing about Geri Lynn—if you ask me, anyway—is that every time she and Scott Bennett, the paper's editor, make out in her parents' basement rec room, Geri draws a little heart in her date book to mark the occasion.

I know this because she showed it to me once. Her date book, I mean. There was a heart on, like, every single page.

Which is kind of funny. I mean that Geri and Scott are even a couple. Because I, and pretty much everybody else on the *Register*'s staff, expected Geri Lynn to be appointed this year's editor in chief—including, I suspect, Geri Lynn herself. I mean, Scott didn't even move to Clayton until this past summer.

Well, that's not quite true. He actually used to live

here . . . we were even in the same fifth grade class. Not that we ever spoke to each other or anything. I mean, you don't talk to members of the opposite sex in the fifth grade. And Scott was never all that talkative to begin with.

But he and I used to check out all the same "uncool" books from the school library. You know, not the popular books, like biographies about Michael Jordan or *Little House on the Prairie* or whatever, but sci-fi/fantasy books like *The Andromeda Strain* or *The Martian Chronicles* or *Fantastic Voyage*. Books the school librarian would frown at while we were checking them out, then go, "Are you sure this is the kind of book you want, dear?" because they weren't exactly on our reading level or whatever.

Not that we ever discussed them with each other or any-thing. The books Scott and I were reading, I mean. I only know he read the same books as I did because whenever I went to check one of them out, Scott's signature was there, right above mine, on the book's checkout card.

Then Scott's parents split up, he moved away with his mom, and I didn't see him again until last summer, when the *Register*'s staff was forced to go to this school-sponsored retreat with our advisor, Mr. Shea, who made us play these trust games so that we could learn to work together as a team. I was just standing there in the parking lot, waiting to board the bus to the retreat, when this car pulled up and guess who got out of it?

Yeah, that'd be Scott Bennett. It turned out he'd decided to give living with his dad a try for a while, and he'd sent in some clippings from his old school's paper, and Mr. Shea had let him on the staff of the *Register*.

And even though it was a little bit like Scott's head had been transplanted onto the body of one of Mrs. Mulvaney's Greek god statues or something, because he was like three feet taller and had turned totally buff since he was, you know, ten, I could tell he was still the same Scott. Because he had a copy of *Dreamcatcher* sticking out of his backpack, which I, of course, had been meaning to read.

By the end of the retreat, Mr. Shea had asked Scott to be editor, because he showed such strong leadership abilities and had also written this totally awesome essay during a free-writing session about being the only guy in this cooking class he'd been forced to take after he'd gotten into some trouble in Milwaukee, where he'd lived with his mom. I guess Scott had been a little bit of a delinquent there or something, acting out and stuff, and the authorities had put him in this new experimental program for kids at risk.

They'd given him a choice: auto shop or cooking class.

Scott had been the only guy in the history of the program to choose the cooking class.

Anyway, in the essay, Scott wrote about how on the first day of class, the cooking teacher had produced a butternut squash and been all, "We're going to make this into soup," and Scott had thought she was yet another huge phony liar, like all the other adults he knew.

And then they ended up making butternut squash soup and it changed Scott's life. He never got in trouble again.

The only problem was, he said, he couldn't seem to stop wanting to cook stuff.

Of course, Scott's essay, good as it was, might not have won him the post of editor in chief if Geri Lynn had been at the retreat to remind Mr. Shea—as she undoubtedly would have, Geri not being shy—that appointing Scott to such an important post wasn't fair, since Geri's a senior and has paid her dues, whereas Scott's still only a junior and new to Clayton High and all.

But Geri had chosen to spend her summer at broadcast journalism camp out in California (yes, it turns out there is such a thing—and Geri Lynn is already so good at schmoozing like Mary Hart on *Entertainment Tonight* that she even got a scholarship to go there), and so she wasn't even at the retreat.

Still, she accepted Mr. Shea's decision pretty graciously. Maybe that's something they teach at TV news camp. You know, how to be gracious about stuff. We didn't actually learn anything like that at the retreat—though we did have a pretty good time making fun of Mr. Shea. Like Mr. Shea had us do this trust exercise that involved getting the whole staff over this log stuck between two trees, seven feet in the air, in the middle of the woods, leaving no one stranded on the other side (did I mention trust exercises are really, really stupid?) without using a ladder or anything, just our hands, because this giant wave of peanut butter was coming down at us.

Did I mention that Mr. Shea's sense of humor is also really, really stupid?

Anyway, when all of us just stood there and looked at Mr. Shea like he was crazy, he went, "Is that too corny?"

And Scott was all, totally deadpan, "Actually, Mr. Shea, it's nutty."

That was when we knew that Scott had all the necessary qualities for the job of editor in chief. Even Geri Lynn— when school started up again in the fall, and she found that she'd lost out on the job she'd wanted so badly—seemed to recognize Scott's superior leadership abilities. At least, the first little heart in her date book appeared there only about a week into the semester, so I guess she isn't holding a grudge about it or anything.

"I think that'd be great," was what Scott said about my idea. You know, of doing a story on the Betty Ann kidnapping.

"It'll be funny. We could do one of those missing person's posters of Betty Ann, like they have in the post office. And offer a reward on Mrs. Mulvaney's behalf."

Geri Lynn stopped jiggling her soda can. When Geri's can stops jiggling, it's a sign everybody should duck. Because Geri's got a temper. I guess they don't offer any training programs about that at broadcast journalism camp.

"That's the stupidest thing I've ever heard," she said. "A *reward*? For the return of a DOLL?"

"But Betty Ann isn't just a doll," Scott said. "She's sort of like the unofficial school mascot."

Which is only true because our real school mascot is so lame. We're the Clayton Roosters. The whole thing is pathetic. Not that it matters, since our school loses every game it plays anyway, in every sport.

But you should see the rooster suit. It's embarrassing, really. Way more embarrassing than having a Cabbage Patch doll for a mascot.

"I think Jen is onto something," Scott said, ignoring Geri's scowl. "Kwang, why don't you write something up?"

Kwang nodded and made a note in his Palm Pilot. I kept my gaze on my notepad, hoping Geri Lynn wasn't mad at me. I mean, I don't consider Geri one of my best friends or anything, but she and I do eat lunch together every day, and besides which we *are* the only girls on the paper (well, except for a couple of freshmen, but, like they even count) and Geri has confided in me a lot—like the thing with the hearts . . . not to mention the fact that Scott is this phenomenal kisser with, like, excellent suckage.

Oh, and that on Sunday mornings, he frequently bakes apple crumble.

I love apple crumble. Geri Lynn, though, won't eat it. She says Scott uses like a whole stick of butter just in the crust and that she can practically feel her arteries hardening just *looking* at it.

Since Geri was already mad at Scott for having agreed to do what she considered such a stupid story in the first place, the fact that he assigned it to Kwang just made her madder.

"For God's sake," Geri said. "It was Jen's idea. Why don't you let Jen write it? Why are you always stealing Jen's ideas and giving them to other people?"

I felt a wave of panic, and shot Scott a look.

But he was totally calm as he said, "Jen's too busy with the layout."

"How do you know?" Geri snarled. "Did you ever bother to ask her?"

I went, "Geri, it's all right. I'm happy with my position on the staff."

Geri snorted like she couldn't believe me. "Puhlease."

I couldn't say what I wanted to, which is that doing

layout is fine by me. That's because I do a lot more for the paper than just that.

Only no one's supposed to know that. Well, no one but Scott, anyway, and Mr. Shea and a few school administrators.

Because one of the other things that had happened on that retreat over the summer was that Mr. Shea had approached me and asked if I'd be willing to take on one of the most sought-after—and secretive—positions on the staff . . . one that for years has traditionally only been held by a senior, but which Mr. Shea felt I was uniquely qualified for, even though I'm only a junior. . . .

And I'd said yes.

# Ask Annie

Dear Annie,

Help! I'm in love with a boy who doesn't know I'm alive. Of course, he has actually never met me, seeing as how he lives 2,000 miles away and works in the entertainment business. Still, when I see him on the big screen, and gaze into his blue eyes, I know that we are soul mates. I am not sure how much longer I can go on without him. But I don't have enough money to buy a plane ticket to L.A., nor do I have anywhere to stay when I get there. Please help me figure out a way to meet my love before he leaves for New Zealand, where he'll be filming his next movie.

Crushed

Dear Crushed,

There is a fine line between celebrity worship and stalking, and you sound ready to cross it. Surrender the fantasy and start concentrating on what's important: finishing school and getting into college.

Besides, you are clearly talking about Luke Striker, and I hear he is still heartbroken over the whole thing with Angelique Tremaine. So get over it.

Annie

*Two*

*Actually, I wasn't* too surprised when Mr. Shea asked me if I'd be the *Register*'s new Annie. That's because for my whole life, people have always come to me with their problems. I don't know why. I mean, it's not like I *want* to hear about Geri Lynn and Scott's love life.

But seemingly since birth I've been cursed with being everybody's confidante. Seriously. I used to think I was a weirdo magnet or something, because it seemed like I could never go anywhere without random strangers coming up to me, telling me all about themselves, like about their hammer collection or their sick ferret or whatever.

But it isn't just random strangers, it turns out. *Everybody* does it. Trina was the first one to put her finger on why. It was her twelfth birthday, and Trina decided to have her birthday party at the Zoom Floom, this giant water slide over in Ellis County. Only on the day of the party, I got my period. Since I was scared of tampons (when you're twelve, those things can be scary. And it wasn't like I had figured out yet to buy the special teen ones—"Petal soft and pinky slim!" I was still trying to jam those super absorbency plus ones of my mom's up in there, and, let me tell you, it wasn't quite working out for me.), I had no choice but to stay home.

But Trina, whom I'd expected to be sympathetic, was anything but. She was all, "I don't care if your stupid pad comes out from under your suit and floats away! You are coming to my party! You HAVE to! You're the mayonnaise!"

I didn't know what Trina was talking about. But it turns out she was more than happy to explain.

"Because you get along with everyone," she told me over the phone that day. "Like mayonnaise. Without mayonnaise, the whole sandwich just falls apart. Like my party's going to if you don't come."

It did, too. Her party, I mean. Elizabeth Gertz accused Kim Doss of copying her because they both ended up wearing identical red J. Crew swimsuits and French braids, and Kim, to prove she had a mind of her own, pushed Elizabeth into the deep part at the base of the waterslide, and she chipped a tooth on the pool's cement floor.

If I had been there, I totally would have intervened before anyone got hurt.

So, you know, it wasn't this huge shock when Mr. Shea handed me the Ask Annie position. Because the person who holds it has to give the people who write in not only good advice but also advice that the school counselor, Ms. Kellogg, will be able to endorse and stand behind.

Which isn't easy. Because Ms. Kellogg is a freak. She is all into yoga and biorhythm and feng shui, and always wants me to tell the people who write in that if they'd move their bedroom mirror so it isn't facing a window or door, they'd stop losing so much karmic energy.

I'm not kidding.

And this is the person who is supposedly going to help me get into a good college someday. Scary.

But Ms. Kellogg and I actually have a pretty good relationship. I listen to her drone on about her macrobiotic diet, and she's always willing to write me a note so I can get out of volleyball in P.E. or whatever.

Anyway, the thing about Ask Annie is, the person who is Annie is supposed to be this huge secret, on account of Annie isn't supposed to have any biases toward certain peer groups, as Ms. Kellogg calls them. Like Annie can't be "known" to be a member of any particular clique, or people will think she can't relate to, like, the problems of someone unpopular like Cara Cow or a jock like Kurt Schraeder or whoever.

Plus, you know, if people knew who Annie was, they might not be willing to write to her at all, since she might guess who the author of the letter was, and spread it around. People don't really do that good a job of disguising their identity when they write to Annie. I mean, maybe they try, but you get people like Trina, who writes to Annie at least once a month about whatever is bugging her (usually it's something about Luke Striker, the love of her life). Trina doesn't even attempt to disguise her handwriting or use a fake e-mail address.

Another reason for the anonymity of Annie is that she is privy to a lot of people's deepest, darkest secrets.

So I have this totally fab position on the paper, but I can't tell anybody about it. I can't even tell Trina or my mom, because they both have the biggest mouths in the entire state of Indiana. I just have to go along, letting them all think I have this very integral role with the paper's layout. Whoopee.

Which is fine. I mean, it's not a big deal. I'm easy.

Except when it comes to people like Geri Lynn. I'd like to tell Geri Lynn. Just so she doesn't keep on thinking Scott is taking advantage of me.

So, anyway, being Annie and all, I get called to Ms. Kellogg's office a lot. She always wants to talk to me about who I think might have written some particularly disturbing letter or e-mail.

Sometimes I know. Sometimes I don't. Sometimes I tell her. Sometimes I don't. I mean, you have to respect a person's right to privacy unless, you know, the person is seriously disturbed.

And fortunately, there are enough people who *want* Ms. Kellogg and the rest of the administration to know their business that they don't really have time to poke their noses into the business of the people who don't.

Like Cara Schlosburg, for instance. Cara totally doesn't care if the whole world knows about her problems. Cara writes *tons* of letters to Annie. I answer all of them, though we don't print them in the paper, because even if we didn't include her signature (she signs each and every one of her letters), everyone would know they were from her anyway. Like a typical one is:

*Dear Annie,*
*Everyone calls me Cara Cow, even though my name is Cara Schlosburg, and they all moo when I walk by them in the hallway. Please help before I do something drastic.*

Only Cara never has done anything drastic yet, that I know of. Once this rumor went around that she had cut herself, and she was out of school for three days. I was really worried she had slit her wrists or something. So I asked my mom to find out what had happened for me, because my mom and Mrs. Schlosburg are in the same aquasize class at the Y.

But it turned out that Cara had given herself a home pedicure and shaved too much dead skin off the soles of her feet and accidentally removed fresh new skin and couldn't walk till it grew back.

That's the kind of thing that happens to Cara. A lot.

It's also the kind of thing that makes my mom go, "You know, Jen, Mrs. Schlosburg is really worried about Cara. She says Cara tries so hard to fit in, but it doesn't seem to do any good. The other kids just keep making fun of her. Maybe if you took her under your wing?"

Of course I can't tell my mom that I *have* taken Cara under my wing. I mean, as Ask Annie.

Anyway, when I got called to the office the day after Kurt Schraeder kidnapped Betty Ann Mulvaney, I figured it was either something to do with a Cara letter or that, alternatively, it had to do with Betty Ann.

Because even though Mrs. Mulvaney had been her typical self about the whole thing, shrugging it off, you could tell it really kind of bothered her. Like I noticed her gaze often strayed toward the place on her desk where Betty Ann used to sit.

And she made this giggling announcement before each class, that if Betty Ann's kidnappers would just return her, there'd be no hard feelings and no questions asked. I had even caught up to Kurt in the lunch line and asked him if he was going to do a ransom note or whatever just because I thought if Mrs. Mulvaney saw the whole thing was a joke, she might feel better about it.

But Kurt was all, "What? A what note?"

So then I had to explain to Kurt, all carefully, about what a ransom note was and how the joke—since that's what I assumed he was doing, kidnapping Betty Ann, and all— would be funnier if he sent Mrs. Mulvaney a note instructing her to, for instance, waive the weekend homework or distribute Brach's caramels to everyone in class, in order to ensure Betty Ann's safe return.

Kurt seemed to really like this idea. It was like it had never occurred to him before. He and his friends went, "Whoa. Genius, man!" and high-fived one another.

Which got me kind of nervous. I mean, these guys weren't the sharpest knives in the drawer. I had no idea how Kurt even got elected senior class president, except, you know, he was the only person who had bothered to run.

So just to be sure they even still *had* Betty Ann, I went, "Kurt, you didn't do anything stupid, did you? Like throw Betty Ann in one of the quarries or something. Did you?"

Kurt looked at me like I was crazy. He went, "Hell, no. I still got her. It's a joke, see? The senior prank, Jen. Heard of it?"

I didn't want Kurt to think I didn't find his prank hilarious. So I just went, "Yeah, funny joke," and grabbed my tacos and ran.

So you can see that when I got called to the office, I pretty much had a feeling that if Cara hadn't locked herself in a toilet stall, crying again, I was probably going to be facing some major grilling on the whereabouts of Betty Ann.

Which would put me, as anyone could see, in a fairly uncomfortable position. I mean, I couldn't side with the administration in the Betty Ann thing, even though I did think it was stupid and wrong of Kurt to take her. But the senior prank—even if it's a terrifically lame one, like Kurt's—is the senior prank, and like a lot of stuff about high school—the SATs and the prom and the pep rallies—you aren't allowed to mess with it, no matter how pointless and dumb you might find it.

So as I dragged myself into Ms. Kellogg's office, I was making all these promises to myself—like how even if they tortured me with the prospect of working in the office all summer, I was going to stick to my guns on the Betty Ann thing and not tell—and I didn't even notice that Ms. Kellogg wasn't the only person in there.

No, Principal Lewis was there, too. And Vice Principal Lucille Thompson—Juicy Lucy, everyone calls her, which is really mean, but the truth is, it sort of fits in an ironic way, because a drier, more sticklike school administrator than Lucille Thompson you really could never imagine.

There was another guy there, too. A guy wearing this shiny gray suit. I should have noticed him straight off—also the fact that he clearly wasn't from around Clayton, since he had a black T-shirt instead of a button-down under his jacket, which is how people in California or New York, not southern Indiana, dress—but I was too worried that I was in trouble.

"Listen, Ms. Kellogg," I said right away, to get it over with. "If it's about Betty Ann, I can't tell you. I mean, I know, of course. I saw the whole thing. But I can't tell you who did it. I really can't. But he promised me Betty Ann's all right, and I'll work on getting her returned in one piece. That's all I can do. I'm sorry. . . ."

That's when I noticed the T-shirt guy . . . not to mention Dr. Lewis and Juicy Lucy. My voice kind of dribbled off.

Ms. Kellogg came to my rescue. I guess she recognized that my chi had been all thrown off by the presence of Dr. Lewis, Juicy Lucy, and a total stranger.

"It's not about Betty Ann, Jen," she said.

"If Miss Greenley knows anything about that doll," Juicy Lucy chimed in, looking upset, "I think she needs to say something, Elaine. Mrs. Mulvaney was very disturbed this morning to see that it was still missing. I understand the

*Register* is doing a story on it, so obviously the paper's staff members know something. It's unconscionable that people's personal items are not safe on their own desks—"

"Never mind about the doll, Lucille," Dr. Lewis said. He had on a short-sleeved shirt and khaki pants. I noticed there were grass stains on them. I think he'd been called in from the course. Whatever this was about, I knew it had to be *big*. They didn't call Dr. Lewis in from the golf course for just anything.

"Jane," he said, "we'd like you to meet—"

"Jen," Ms. Kellogg corrected him.

Only nobody ever corrects Dr. Lewis, so he blinked like he didn't know what she was talking about.

"Jane," Dr. Lewis started again. "This is John Mitchell. John, this is Jane Greenley."

"How do you do, Jane," Mr. Mitchell said. He held out his hand. I shook it. "Nice to meet you."

"Nice to meet you, too," I said.

I sounded calm enough, I guess, but inside my head, thoughts were spinning around like the Tilt-A-Whirl at the county fair. What was going on? Who was this guy? How much trouble was I in? Did this have something to do with me putting that I wanted to be a drill press operator on the state achievement test? Because I was seriously only kidding around about that. Trina had done it, too. And was this going to be over by lunch? Because I only get twenty-five minutes to eat.

"Jane," Dr. Lewis went on, "Mr. Mitchell here has just arranged for Clayton High School to receive a great honor. A very great honor."

"Some honor," Juicy Lucy said with a snort. Dr. Lewis shot her a warning look, but Miss Thompson didn't take the hint. In fact, she got defensive.

"Well, I'm not going to sit here and lie, Richard," she said. "It's completely ridiculous. We're supposed to drop everything—disrupt all our students—and for what?"

"We hope there won't be any disruption at all, Miss Thompson," Mr. Mitchell said. "And of course the minute there appears to be—"

"There won't be any disruption, Jui—I mean, Lucille," Ms. Kellogg said. I'd once let slip to her what everybody calls Miss Thompson behind her back, and ever since then, Ms. Kellogg had been incapable of calling her boss anything else. "That's the whole point. They want this to go as smoothly as possible—"

"Well, I don't see how they can expect it to." Juicy—I mean, Miss Thompson's—lips practically disappeared, she had them pressed together so hard. "The boy is going to be mobbed the minute he sets foot on campus. Those girls . . . they don't have the slightest bit of control over themselves.

Did you see what Courtney Deckard was wearing today? A halter top. To school! I made her call her mother and ask her to bring over something decent to wear for the rest of the day."

Both Dr. Lewis and Mr. Mitchell stared at Miss Thompson as if she had just sucked all the available oxygen out of the room. In a way, I think maybe she had. I know *I* felt a little light-headed.

"I can assure you," Mr. Mitchell went on, "that that isn't going to happen. Because Mr. Striker is going to keep a very low profile. And he's going to be wearing a disguise."

"A disguise." Miss Thompson rolled her eyes. "Oh, *that* will help."

"You'd be amazed," Mr. Mitchell said, "what a simple pair of glasses can do."

"Oh," Juicy Lucy said, throwing her hands into the air. "Well, *glasses*. Why didn't you say so? That'll fool them."

"Excuse me," I said. Because I was really curious to find out what was going on. It didn't appear to have anything to do with Cara or Betty Ann. In fact, unless I was way off base, it seemed to have something to do with— "Do you mean *Luke* Striker?"

Ms. Kellogg grinned, and started to nod like a maniac. "Yes," she said. "Yes, yes. Luke Striker. He's coming here. To Clayton High School."

I looked at her like she was nuts. Actually, this is how I normally look at Ms. Kellogg. Because most of the time, I think she *is* nuts.

"Luke Striker," I repeated. "Luke Striker, the star of *Heaven Help Us?*"

Which used to be like one of the most popular shows on television, back when there were no reality shows. I used to watch it. Luke Striker, who played a preacher's kid, had grown up on the show, getting seriously hotter every season. Hot enough that he ended up leaving the show to pursue a film career and had managed to get cast as Tarzan in the latest Tarzan movie, in which he'd been quite . . .

Well, naked.

Then he'd gone on to play Lancelot in the latest Camelot movie. . . .

And had done pretty well in them both, too. At least, so far as diehard fans like Trina were concerned.

The fans weren't as excited over what was going on in Luke Striker's personal life, however. Rumor had it—at least according to Trina, who'd talked about it ad nauseam all winter—that Luke had embarked on a torrid romance with his *Lancelot and Guenevere* co-star Angelique Tremaine. They were even supposed to have had each other's names tattooed on their biceps at some kind of commitment ceremony. You know, instead of wedding rings.

Only I guess Angelique hadn't followed through with her part of the commitment, because not even six months ago, Angelique had up and married some French film director twice her age, behind Luke's back! Trina had been exultant—though sad for Luke, of course. Because now he's free—brokenhearted, according to the tabloids—but free. Free to fall in love with Trina.

And now it appeared that Luke Striker, star of the silver screen and lover scorned, was coming to Clayton, Indiana.

"He's been cast as a midwestern high school senior in his next film," Mr. Mitchell explained pleasantly, "a riveting drama of love and betrayal in the Hoosier heartland. Since Luke grew up in L.A.—you know, he started working on *Heaven Help Us* when he was just seven—he feels he needs to immerse himself in Indiana high school culture in order to lend authenticity to his role—"

"Isn't that amazing?" Ms. Kellogg asked, her eyes shining. "Who knew he was such a true artist, so dedicated to his craft?"

Um, not me. I mean, you certainly couldn't tell from that Doritos commercial he'd done that was aired during last year's Super Bowl.

"So . . ." I looked from Mr. Mitchell to Ms. Kellogg and back again. "Luke Striker is coming to *Clayton*?"

"Just for two weeks," Mr. Mitchell said, "to research this

role he's playing. And he specifically requested—or at least, the studio specifically requested—that his true identity be kept strictly confidential. Luke doesn't feel he can have an authentic high school experience if he's got hordes of fans following him around."

"Which is where we thought you could help us out, Jen," Ms. Kellogg chimed in, still looking starry-eyed. "See, we're planning on having Mr. Striker pose as a transfer student with the name Lucas Smith."

"Uh-huh," I said. Now that I knew I wasn't there to defend Cara or be grilled about the abduction of Betty Ann, I was only half listening—for one thing, because I'm not as into celebrities and stuff as, say, Trina is and for another, because I was missing Troubadours, and Mr. Hall always gets kind of peevish when I'm called out of class. Not because I'm this huge integral part of the choir or anything, but because I still need to work on my arm movements before Luers, that show choir invitational we're supposed to go to at the end of next week. I just can't seem to get the whole jazz hands thing right.

"So what we were suggesting to Mr. Mitchell, Jen," Ms. Kellogg was going on, "is that—well, because you're so good at keeping secrets, and we know we can count on you not to blow this one or get silly about it—you could be assigned to be Luke's student guide. You know how we like to give transfer students a guide to help them out their first few days. And you could take Luke around with you to all of your classes—show him the ropes, so to speak. Answer his questions, maybe help deflect anyone who gets too suspicious. . . . Then he can, you know, soak in the atmosphere here at Clayton without anyone suspecting that he is who he really is. How does that sound?"

Truthfully? It sounded like a load of horse manure. I mean, did they really think no one was going to notice that the new guy looks exactly like Luke Striker? Did they honestly think calling him Lucas Smith was going to throw everyone—especially someone like Trina, who worships the guy—off? I really thought Mr. Mitchell, the administration, and Luke Striker himself were underestimating the intelligence of my fellow Clayton High students.

But, hey, it wouldn't be the first time.

I shrugged. I mean, what was I going to say? No?

"Sure," I said. "Fine. Whatever."

Ms. Kellogg smiled in a pleased way and shot what looked to me like a triumphant glance at Juicy Lucy. I mean, Miss Thompson.

"See?" Ms. Kellogg said. "I told you so. You can always count on Jen not to make a fuss."

Which is totally true.

# *Ask Annie*

Ask Annie your most complex interpersonal relationship questions. Go on, we dare you! All letters to Annie are subject to publication in the Clayton High School *Register*. Names and e-mail addresses of correspondents guaranteed confidential.

Dear Annie,

I tell my best friend everything. I even tell her about the dreams I have at night. But she never seems to open up to me—even about important things, like who she likes and stuff like that. I don't feel like we really have the open, engaging relationship that I'd like. What can I do to let her know it's safe to confide in me?

Feeling Unloved

Dear Unloved,

Your friend may have nothing to confide. Not everyone finds her own dreams as gripping as you evidently find yours. Maybe she's just trying not to bore everyone. Why don't you return the favor?

Annie

*Three*

*Mr. Mitchell said* I had to tell my parents. Because of my being a minor and all. Which I didn't really get, since it wasn't like Luke and I would be *dating* or anything. I mean, I was just going to be showing him where the gym was and not to take the glazed carrots in the caf. But whatever.

Mr. Mitchell offered to do it himself—talk to my parents—but I told him I'd do it. I knew if he did it, my parents would blow the whole thing out of proportion. Like the Ask Annie thing.

I waited until after dinner to do it, when my brothers went off to do their homework. I have two little brothers— Cal and Rick, in eighth and sixth grade. Cal's a jock—he plays every sport except football, which my mom won't let him play, because she thinks it's too dangerous. Because of this, of course, Cal's goal is to pursue a career in law enforcement, preferably the SWAT team. Rick, in contrast, hates sports. He wants to be a child star like Luke Striker used to be. He doesn't understand why our parents won't get him an agent. They've tried explaining to him that there are no agents in Clayton, Indiana, but Rick doesn't care. He says his time is running out and pretty soon he won't be cute anymore so somebody better discover him, quick.

Like me, my brothers get along with pretty much everybody . . . even with me and with each other, except for the occasional burst of acrimony over possession of the remote or the last chocolate fudge Pop-Tart or whatever.

Still, I decided it was probably best to keep them in the dark about the Luke Striker thing, because they might not be able to keep it to themselves. Cal's got an old Luke Striker—aka Tarzan—action figure, after all. And Rick would probably try to get his agent's phone number.

Because I was so casual about it—"There's this actor and he's coming to town to research a role and they want me to show him around school"—my parents both just sort of shrugged when they heard the news. Only my dad looked alarmed, and that was just for a minute—and not even, as I initially thought, because he'd heard about the Angelique-tattoo thing.

"He's not staying with us, is he?" he asked, looking over the top of the paper he was reading—the *Clayton Gazette*, which comes in the afternoon, not morning, so the reporters don't have to go to work too early. My town's really small. Did I mention that already?

"No, Dad," I said. "He's renting a condo at the lake."

"Thank God," my dad said, and disappeared back behind the paper. My dad can't stand houseguests.

"Who is this boy again?" my mom wanted to know.

"Luke Striker," I said. "He used to be on *Heaven Help Us*. He played the oldest son."

My mom smiled. "Oh, that sweet blond one?"

I wondered if my mom would still think Luke was sweet if she'd seen him in the lagoon scene in *Tarzan*. The one where his loin pelt had kind of floated away, thrilling Jane— and Trina—very much.

"That's the one," I said.

"Well," my mom said, as she turned back to her sketch pad. "I hope you don't get a crush on him. Because you know, he lives all the way out in Hollywood. I doubt you two will see all that much of each other after he leaves."

"No worries, Mom," I said, thinking about the commitment ceremony tattoos. "Luke Striker really isn't my type."

"Well, Trina, then," my mom said. "You know how Trina is."

"Yeah," I said. I knew exactly how Trina was. "But he's supposed to be wearing glasses the whole time or something. Nobody's supposed to be able to recognize him."

"That's ridiculous," Mom said.

"I don't see why." My dad turned to the homes section of the paper. He's an architect and likes to see what kind of houses are selling every week. "It worked for Clark Kent."

My obligations to my family met, I went upstairs to my room to start my own homework. I turned on my computer and found a slew of e-mails, most of them from Trina. Even though she lives right next door, we still e-mail each other more than we talk on the phone . . . more than we talk in person, even. I don't know why. Maybe because we don't leave our houses all that much. There aren't a whole lot of places to go in Clayton. Besides school, that is. And I'm always reading, and Trina's always practicing for whatever role she's going out for in drama.

In fact, you can usually hear her practicing in her room, because our houses are like a hundred feet away. Trina has what Mr. Hall calls a very strong diaphragm. It allows for a lot of vocal projection. She's gotten the lead in just about every play that's ever been put on in the Clayton school system, so I guess she's got a good shot at a career. Her plan is to go to Yale Drama School, like her idol, Meryl Streep. Then she says she's going to take Broadway by storm. Trina has no interest in film work. She says the interaction between an artist and the audience during a live performance is an opiate to which she's become addicted.

*Hey, where'd you disappear to during choir?* Trina wrote. Her online name is—no surprise—Dramaqueen. *La Hall about had a fit, you were gone so long.*

I have gotten pretty used to lying to Trina about the whole Ask Annie thing—she flat out accused me of being Annie once, when the *Register* printed a letter from a kid who claimed he couldn't stay awake without drinking a six-pack of Diet Coke, and then had to swallow like four Sominex at night to go to sleep. My response, "So quit drinking so much soda," was apparently so "classically Jen"— at least according to Trina—that I nearly blew my cover.

So it wasn't really any skin off my teeth to reply,

**JENNYG:** Oh, Cara had another cow. What'd I miss?

**DRAMAQUEEN:** That girl must be starved for attention at home. Why else does she try so hard to get it at school? Anyway, you fully missed it. La Hall showed us the dress we're supposed to order to wear at Luers. Get ready: It's red with a sequined lightning bolt down the front.

This was appalling. I mean, considering it was going on my body.

J E N N Y G : You lie.

D R A M A Q U E E N : *Au contraire, mon frère.* AND it contains not a single fiber naturally occurring in nature. AND it costs a hundred and eighty bucks.

J E N N Y G : *Verberat nos et lacerat fortuna!*

D R A M A Q U E E N : You're not kidding. The guys have it easy. They just have to get red cummerbunds and bow ties to go with their tuxes. We're having a car wash Saturday to raise fundage for those girls whom *fortuna* has forsaken. I signed you up for the twelve-to-two shift. I figured at least we could work on our tans while we wash. Provided it doesn't rain.

J E N N Y G : You know, you neglected to mention when I signed up for this class that it was going to begin eating away at my social calender, bit by excruciating bit.

D R A M A Q U E E N : Oh, like you have something better to do.

Sadly, this is true. I don't have anything better to do. Still.

J E N N Y G : A HUNDRED AND EIGHTY BUCKS? For a dress I'm never going to wear again? That is RIDICULOUS.

D R A M A Q U E E N : That's showbiz.

J E N N Y G : And I thought the padded bras were bad . . .

D R A M A Q U E E N : Seriously. Hey, so guess what? Steve asked me to the Spring Fling.

Steve McKnight is Trina's boy toy. He sings baritone in the Troubadours and played Henry II to Trina's Eleanor of Aquitaine in the Drama Club's version of *The Lion in Winter*. Steve's also been Beauregard to Trina's Auntie Mame, Romeo to her Juliet, and so on. Trina isn't in love with him— she is saving herself for Luke Striker—but since he's taller than she is, and head over heels for her, she lets him take her out. That way she gets to see all the new movies in town. For free.

Trina is fairly morally bankrupt, but I can't help liking her anyway. It bugs me, though, when she dumps Steve— which she does almost every time she gets a date with someone else—because I'm always the one he comes running to, wanting to know what he did to make her mad.

I was happy to hear they were going to the spring

formal—also known as the Spring Fling—together. It would mean a lot to Steve. And then Trina could tell me all about it. Since I'll never find out on my own, no one having asked me and all.

JENNYG: Lucky.

DRAMAQUEEN: Why don't you find some guy to take you, and we can, you know, double?

JENNYG: Oh, okay. Let me just check—oh, yeah, sorry, nobody's in love with me this week.

DRAMAQUEEN: That's because you're too nice to everyone.

JENNYG: Yeah. Because most guys look for emotionally abusive girls to go out with.

DRAMAQUEEN: I mean it. You're like nice to *everyone*. You treat all guys the same. So how are they supposed to know if you think of them as just a friend or as a potential *amor*? That has to be why no one's ever asked you out. I mean, it's not like you're ugly.

JENNYG: Hey. Thanks. That means so much.

Actually, I know I'm not ugly. I'm no Catrina Larssen, but I do have this wholesome girl-next-door thing going for me. You know the drill: brown hair, hazel eyes, freckles—the whole bit. It's kind of sickening, actually. I've been trying to grow my bangs out, though, to make up for it.

DRAMAQUEEN: I'm serious. I mean, you could have had Scott Bennett, but you blew it.

Trina has this weird idea that Scott Bennett is the perfect guy for me. That's because when I got back from the *Register* retreat, I guess I sort of talked about him a lot. But just because we'd had so much fun. Like a lot of nights, he and I ended up sitting next to each other at the campfire, arguing about whether or not the film *Total Recall* did justice to the Philip K. Dick short story it was based on, or if H. G. Wells or Isaac Asimov was the true father of science fiction.

And I might have mentioned to her how, on the way home from camp, the bus stopped for lunch at an Outback Steakhouse, Scott kept calling the waitress by her name. You know, the one printed on her name tag. Like he'd go, "What would you recommend, Rhonda?" and "We've decided on the onion blossom, Rhonda," and "Thanks for the refill, Rhonda." I don't know why, but I couldn't stop laughing. At one point I laughed so hard I almost choked, and Kwang had to pound me on the back.

But I guess what really made Trina think Scott was perfect for me was when I told her about the log. The one between the two trees that we all had to get across, before the wall of peanut butter killed us. Not the part about Scott's joke—"It's nutty, actually"—but the part about how Scott and I were the last two people on the one side of the log, and how he'd picked me up so that I could grab it—the log, I mean—and swing over the top.

I must have mentioned to Trina how effortlessly Scott had seemed to lift me—like I didn't weigh a thing—and how I'd kind of noticed his arm muscles bulging under the sleeves of his T-shirt. And how he'd smelled sort of nice. And how his hands were . . . you know. Kind of big. And strong.

Which was a mistake—to tell Trina, I mean—because then she kept thinking I liked Scott—you know, *that* way— and bugging me to ask him out. To the movies or something. She said it was obvious we were destined for each other and that if I didn't ask him out we'd never get together, since he'd just go on thinking that I liked him as a friend, because that's how I treat all boys, not being a flirt like her.

Which is ridiculous—about Scott and I being destined for each other—because it's totally obvious that Scott and Geri Lynn are perfect together. I mean, look how fast they hooked up. The first day of school, practically. At least according to the hearts in Geri's date book.

It's a good thing Trina is planning on a career in the theater, because as a matchmaker she's got a lot to learn.

I've mentioned this to her numerous times, but that doesn't seem to stop her from trying.

DRAMAQUEEN: Okay, maybe things didn't work out with Scott, but that's no reason to give up on men. You're very cute. I'm sure Steve could get one of the other baritones to take you out. Or maybe one of the tenors . . .

JENNYG: STOP. WAIT. DON'T.

DRAMAQUEEN: Okay, okay. But there has to be SOMEONE you like.

JENNYG: Hey, there's nobody YOU like. Why do *I* have to like someone, and you don't?

DRAMAQUEEN: Because, *pulchera*, I'm saving myself for Luke Striker.

Oooh. For the first time, it occurred to me if word about Luke's true identity got out, it could affect me in a highly personal manner. You know, in the form of my best friend losing her virginity before me. Providing Luke turned out to like her back, I mean.

I have to admit, I felt a twinge of guilt. Over the whole keeping-Luke-Striker's-impending-visit-to-our-fair-city thing from Trina. She was going to be plenty mad when she found out the truth.

But then again, Trina has never really managed to stay mad at me long.

Trina and I were e-mailing the answers to our Latin homework back and forth—which isn't cheating, exactly. We were just confirming that we'd gotten the same thing, when I got a message from someone who wasn't Trina or Geri Lynn or any of the people who normally e-mail me. This person's screen name was Otempora, which we learned in Latin is a phrase meaning, "What an age we live in!" as if they had to worry about stuff like al-Qaeda and J. Lo back in the year 9.

Otempora happens to be Scott Bennett's screen name.

I clicked on the message right away, figuring it was probably something related to the newspaper.

It wasn't.

O T E M P O R A : Hey, Jen. You aren't mad that I gave your story idea to Kwang, were you? The one about Betty Ann's kidnapping?

I could tell Geri Lynn had been harping at him about it. Lately, it seems, Geri's been harping at Scott more than ever. I personally think it's because Geri is graduating and going off to college. In California. To major in broadcast journalism. Talk about a big change. I've noticed that sometimes, when people are going away, they pick fights with you for no reason. It's like it's easier for them to say good-bye if they're mad at you than if they still like you. Trina does this to me every time she and her parents leave for their summer house on Lake Wawasee. It's kind of funny.

Of course, I couldn't tell Scott this. You know—that his girlfriend was just picking a fight because she's so upset about leaving him. Because it isn't actually any of my business. And besides, he hadn't asked. Instead, I wrote:

JENNYG: Of course I'm not mad. Why would I be mad?

Scott wrote back.

OTEMPORA: Yeah, that's what I thought. But Geri thinks you're mad. Of course, she doesn't know exactly how much you've got on your plate—

No, Geri doesn't. Because she, like the rest of the world, has no idea I'm Annie.

O T E M P O R A : —but you would think she'd know you well enough by now to know you aren't the type of girl who gets mad about stuff like that.

No, I'm not. I'm not that type of girl at all.

I told him not to worry about it, then turned to my trig homework. Because even not-that-type-of-girls have to do their homework.

Even girls who, unbeknownst to the rest of the world, are about to become close personal friends with a big star like Luke Striker.

# Ask Annie

Ask Annie your most complex interpersonal relationship questions. Go on, we dare you! All letters to Annie are subject to publication in the Clayton High School *Register*. Names and e-mail addresses of correspondents guaranteed confidential.

Dear Annie,

I only like guys who are taken. You know, guys who already have girlfriends. I flirt with them until they dump whoever they're dating, and then as soon as they're available, I start not to like them anymore. What is up with this? And what can I do to stop it?

Wannabe Ur Girlfriend—Until I Am

Dear Wannabe Girlfriend,

You either fear commitment or get a thrill out of stealing someone else's guy. Either way, the fact that you recognize that it's a problem means you are more than halfway there as far as solving it goes. Make a conscious effort to keep your mitts off your friends' guys . . . because if you don't, they won't be your friends for long, and pretty soon, you won't have ANY friends, male _or_ female.

Annie

*Four*

*I'd expected Luke* Striker to show up sometime
the next week, or maybe the week after. I certainly didn't
expect him to arrive in Clayton the very next *day*.

But that's exactly what happened. I was just sitting there
in Latin, waiting for class to begin and scanning my copy of
the newest *Register*, when all of a sudden the door opened,
Ms. Kellogg peeked in, said my name, then crooked a finger
at me.

I slid out from behind my desk and went out into the hall
to join her and the tall, scruffy-looking person standing
beside her.

"Jenny," Ms. Kellogg said, her eyes shining more brightly
than usual. "This is Lucas Smith, the new transfer student
we talked to you about yesterday."

I'd been so absorbed in Kwang's story about Betty
Ann—I have to admit, my layout job looked particularly

good: There was a great photo of Betty Ann in her Clayton High cheerleader uniform with the words MISSING: REWARD underneath it, just like on the back of a milk carton—that at first I was almost like *What transfer student?*

Then I remembered. Luke Striker. Luke Striker was coming to Clayton to research a role, and he was going to pose as a transfer student.

And there he was.

Even though nobody was paying the slightest bit of attention to Ms. Kellogg or "Lucas," I felt myself starting to turn beet red with embarrassment. The second bell hadn't rung yet, so most people were still scurrying around the hallway, not even looking toward us. I don't know why I was so mortified.

I certainly hadn't expected to feel this way. I mean, about seeing Luke Striker in the flesh. Or actually not even, since he had *way* more clothes on than he'd had in his last movie. Someone must have tipped him off about how boys in Indiana dressed, since he had the look down—baggy jeans, oversize football jersey, a pair of those really ugly cross trainers. He'd added to these a pair of wire-rimmed glasses, plus it looked as if he'd been growing his hair out. It was even longer than when he'd played Lancelot. And darker. Apparently, Luke's not exactly a natural blond.

And he was taller than I thought he'd be. The guy standing there in the doorway, this guy who I was supposed to be in charge of "showing the ropes," actually looked no more like a movie star than I did. . . .

Except, of course, if you knew he was one.

"Oh," I said lamely, since Ms. Kellogg just kept standing there, looking down at me all expectantly, smiling her giddiest smile. "Yeah. Hi."

Luke just nodded at me. I couldn't tell if he was trying to be merciful, on account of he'd noticed my flaming cheeks or was just, you know, naturally cool. In any case, it was clear that I was about as interesting to him as an old rerun of *Heaven Help Us.*

"Well," Ms. Kellogg said, "I trust you'll help Mrs. Mulvaney find, er, Lucas a seat. And that you'll show him around. Right, Jen?"

"Sure," I managed to croak. What was *wrong* with me? I swear I am *so* not the type to be impressed by celebrities. All the celebrities I like aren't technically even celebrities . . . you know, like authors, like Stephen King or Tolkien or whoever.

And here I was blushing because *Luke Striker* had nodded at me?

Something was wrong. Very wrong.

"Great," Ms. Kellogg said. The second bell rang. Behind the lenses of his glasses, Luke winced, as if the sound hurt his head.

"Well, I'll just leave you here, then, er, Lucas," Ms. Kellogg said. People were starting to stream into the classroom—or trying to, anyway. It was kind of hard, with us blocking the doorway the way we were. "All of your teachers should be aware that you're, uh, here. We sent around a memo late yesterday."

"Great," Luke said. From behind him, I could hear Mrs. Mulvaney crying, "*Eo! Eo!*" which means *go*, or in this case, *Get out of the way*.

We got out of the way. Mrs. Mulvaney finally made it into the classroom. I noticed that she didn't look at Ms. Kellogg or Luke, even though they'd been blocking her way. At least, not right away. Instead, her gaze went directly to the spot where Betty Ann had been.

Seeing that the doll was still gone, Mrs. Mulvaney turned her attention to the newcomers . . . but not before I saw her face twitch, just a little. I was more sure than ever that she missed Betty Ann. I mean, *really* missed her.

"Mrs. Mulvaney, this is that new pupil we spoke about, Lucas Smith," Ms. Kellogg said. "The one Jenny will be student guiding?"

"Oh, of course," Mrs. Mulvaney said, showing no sign that she'd guessed Luke's true identity. Probably because she hadn't. Latin teachers aren't usually all that in touch with popular culture. "Let's have everyone behind Jen move back a seat—there's an empty desk over by the pencil sharpener. That's it."

Luke sank down into the seat behind me. I had to hand it to him. He even had the whole I-am-so-not-thrilled-to-be-here walk thing down. His posture and gait were indiscernible from those of Kurt Schraeder and his friends, when they came strolling in a few seconds later, just before the third and final bell.

Mrs. Mulvaney introduced the new pupil to the rest of the class—in Latin—and we all dutifully greeted our new *amicus*. Luke raised one hand and went, "Yo," in a bored voice.

Even his voice, I was mortified to note, made me blush!

As soon as Mrs. Mulvaney turned away, Luke stabbed me in the back with his pencil (eraser-end first, thank God) and whispered in my ear, "You seriously have class this early *every day*?"

It took a few seconds for the meaning behind his words to sink in. That was because chills were going all up and down my spine. Having a movie star like Luke Striker whisper in your ear? I'm telling you, my *mom* would have gotten chills.

I was trying hard to act cool about the whole thing, though. I whispered back, "Um, yes."

"But it's, like, *eight*," Luke said with some incredulity.

"I know," I whispered back. Then, trying to be encouraging, I added, "But we get out at three."

"*Three!* That's seven hours from now."

Luke's breath tickled my cheek. It smelled like he'd just downed a Listerine strip. I wondered if all movie stars walk around with such minty fresh breath. Maybe that's what sets them apart, you know, from the rest of us. Naturally nice-smelling breath.

"Um," I said, trying to keep my wits about me. But all I could manage to come up was a witty, "I know."

Luke sank back in his desk in disbelief. "Holy—"

Mrs. Mulvaney, who heard this last part, turned around and asked Luke and me, in Latin, if there was a problem. I told her there wasn't.

But there was. Oh, yes, there was. Because I wasn't expecting Luke to be such a complete and utter hottie in real life. Not, you know, that I'd thought his on-screen hotness had all been special effects, or whatever . . .

Except that I guess maybe I had.

But it wasn't.

And I wasn't the only girl in school who noticed. Seriously. Luke followed me everywhere—to my locker, to class, to the water fountain. And though nobody recognized him— nobody even went, "Hey, you know who you look like? Luke Striker"—I noticed that the gazes of the female population of

Clayton High School seemed glued to the guy. He couldn't lift a hand to so much as smooth away a lock of hair that had fallen into his eyes without causing half the people in my English class to catch their breath.

The guy was *hot.* There was no getting around it. I didn't blame Angelique for the tattoo one little bit.

The only thing I couldn't figure out was why she'd dumped him.

Although I can't say I noticed that Luke was much of a conversationalist. He barely spoke three words to me all morning. I couldn't figure out if it was because he's just by nature a quiet guy or if he was mad at me or something. Except that I hadn't done anything that I knew of to make him mad. It wasn't until, trailing after me to second period trig, I got a clue as to what the problem might be when he asked blearily, "Look, is there someplace around here I can get an espresso?"

"Espresso?" Can I just say that *espresso* is not a word you hear a lot in Clayton? I tried to be nice about it though. "Well, there's a Starbucks downtown."

"You mean I gotta *drive* somewhere if I want to get a coffee?" Luke's blue eyes—so gorgeous on screen but in real life (even when hidden behind glasses) even more impressive, like twin swimming pools, they were so blue—widened. "What is *with* this place?"

"Well, nothing, really," I said. "I mean . . . it's high school."

Luke pretty much slept through trig and French. He didn't start waking up, really, until around fourth period. Which was good, because that's when I had Troubadours. Luke was going to have to be on his toes around Trina. Because if anyone was going to see through his "disguise," it was Trina.

I warned him about her on our way to the music wing. The more time I spent around him, the less tongue-tied I was becoming.

But that didn't mean I was, you know, exactly *at ease* in his presence. Because I still hadn't exactly figured him out. Which is weird, because I'm usually pretty good at that sort of thing.

"If you really want to stick with this anonymity thing," I said to him, "you're gonna totally have to watch your step around Trina. She's got theatrical aspirations. And she has every episode of *Heaven Help Us* memorized, practically."

Luke wasn't even paying attention to me. He'd finally opened his eyes wide enough to spy the soda machine.

"Caffeine!" he said, and practically threw himself on it. Then his face fell. "I don't have any change!"

I fished a dollar out of my jeans and handed it to him.

"I'm serious, Luke," I said, as kids poured into the band

room behind us. "Trina's my best friend. I know what I'm talking about."

I've never seen anyone drink an entire can of Coke without pausing for breath. But Luke Striker managed it. When he was done, he let out a gentle burp and tossed the empty can over his head—backward—at the nearby trash can.

And made it.

"No problem," he said in the most animated voice he'd used all morning.

Then he smiled. And I felt my insides give a lurch. Not a good sign.

After the soda, Luke perked up a lot. And when we entered the choir room, which is like this sunken pit of carpeted risers in slowly descending steps, he even visibly brightened at the sight of his reflection in the wall of mirrors on the far side of the room, where we're supposed to watch ourselves breathe. Or at least, those of us whose views aren't impeded by Karen Sue Walters's hair.

It was right then that Trina came in. I could tell she must have already heard about the new guy I was student guiding, since she looked all around the room and then, when her gaze fell on me and Luke, she got a very determined expression on her face and came barreling down the steps toward us, going, "So, Jen, aren't you going to introduce me to your new *friend*?"

"Trina," I said quickly. "Hi. This is Lucas Smith. Lucas, this is my friend Trina."

It was at that point that Luke turned around and said to Trina, "Hi. You're the actress, right?"

Trina looked up at Luke—he was pretty tall, over six feet—and practically melted into a puddle right in front of him.

"Why," she said, in a voice I'd never heard her use before. "Yes. That's me."

"Nice to meet you," Luke said. "So what's the theater department like here? Is it any good?"

I wanted to elbow Luke and be all, *Cool it on the theater stuff,* because I was afraid Trina would make the connection—Lucas Smith . . . theater . . . *Luke Striker.*

But I guess I overestimated Trina's obsession with the guy, since she just started going off about how it was a shame he'd transferred too late to audition for the spring musical and how the local paper had called her portrayal of Auntie Mame "inspired" and how lucky Lucas was that Mr. Hall had let him into Troubadours at all, that the audition process had been really arduous. . . .

Which made me wonder how Dr. Lewis had worked that—talked Mr. Hall into letting a guy who hadn't even auditioned into his precious show choir, I mean—and if Mr. Hall had maybe been let in on the truth. Although it's true that Mr. Hall is pretty exasperated with the tenors. Kind of like he is with my dancing.

It was at this point that Steve—the baritone who is so in love with Trina that he willingly sits through whole romantic comedies at the mall's cineplex just so he can be close to her for ninety minutes—came up to us.

"Hey," he said. Steve is kind of on the skinny side, with a sticky-outy Adam's apple. When he gets nervous, that Adam's apple bobs up and down. It was bobbing like crazy as he came up to Trina and Luke. "What's up?"

"Oh, hi, Steve," Trina said in an offhand way. "This is Lucas."

"Hi," Steve said to Luke.

"Hey, man," Luke said back, outcooling Steve with just two words and a nod. Poor Steve!

"All right, people!" Mr. Hall came out of his office, which was attached to the choir room, and clapped his hands. "Seats, please. Take your seats!" Then his gaze fell on Luke. "You. Who are you?"

It was kind of funny to see him meet Luke Striker. It was obvious now that Mr. Hall had no idea who he was being introduced to.

But I mean, here was this guy who was a real actor—had made millions at it—and then here was Mr. Hall, who had told us that he used to work on Broadway, but who now directed a high school choir in southern Indiana.

And yet the choir director was acting way snottier than the actor. Mr. Hall immediately started going off about how he'd gotten the memo about Luke and all, but that he really resented the assumption on the part of the administration that just anybody could be a Troubadour, and that Luke (Lucas) should have had to audition like everybody else, and that Mr. Hall didn't see why he should let him in without one, just because it was so late in the school year.

Luke didn't so much as blink an eye. Probably because he's used to directors and their absurd demands and all. He just went, "Oh, don't worry, sir, I'll just observe until I catch on."

I think it was the *sir* that really did the trick. Just like Trina, Mr. Hall was instantly charmed. He even let Luke sit by the accompanist and turn pages.

I have to admit, I was pretty impressed at how Luke had buttered up Mr. Hall.

But I didn't have a whole lot of time during fourth period to think about Luke. That's because Mr. Hall made us run through our Luers program three whole times. I mean, we had to stand up and do the arm movements and everything. It bummed me out that I couldn't hide behind Karen Sue Walters's hair and read anymore. It bummed me out even more that the arm motions were really complicated and hard to remember, and that I kept messing up and Mr. Hall kept yelling at me.

"You're behind, Miss Greenley!" and "Stop sloughing off, Jenny!" was all I heard all class period.

Trina was really making me sweat it for those extracurricular points, let me tell you.

We altos don't have it as bad as the sopranos, though. They actually have to DANCE. With HATS. Seriously. They have to do like a hat-and-cane routine to "All That Jazz" from *Chicago*, only without the canes. Which is actually fine by them, because the sopranos are all good dancers. But we altos have to pass them the hats from this stack hidden behind the risers. It's super hard . . . you know, for somebody like me with no sense of rhythm. By the time the bell rang for lunch, I was exhausted.

But Luke, it turned out, was just starting to get revved up.

"You guys actually get school credit for that?" Luke wanted to know, as we were leaving the choir room.

It's kind of funny that he figured out show choir was lame so fast. I mean, I'd been in the choir for three whole months before I figured it out. It's not just the padded bras. "All That Jazz" is the coolest number we do. The rest of our program consists of what Mr. Hall calls Broadway show-stoppers, which include "As Long as He Needs Me" from *Oliver* (we altos especially like the line "As long as he needs me/I'll cling on steadfastly." We sing it as "Klingon." So far Mr. Hall hasn't noticed) and "Day by Day" from *Godspell*.

No, the lamest part is that Mr. Hall makes us travel around and perform in elementary schools and at Kiwanis meetings and stuff. I'm totally serious. I was horrified when I found out. I wanted to kill Trina. But by then it was too late; there were no more spaces open in any other classes for Ms. Kellogg to switch me into.

In a way show choir isn't that bad, though, because it gives the school's most sensitive artist types a place where they can feel safe. A bunch of Troubadours actually eat lunch in the choir room, just so they don't have to face the Kurt Schraeders of the school down in the caf.

That isn't why Trina always wants to eat in the choir room, though. She just wants to make sure Mr. Hall—who lunches in his office, instead of the teacher's lounge; I don't think Mr. Hall is very popular with the rest of the faculty— doesn't hand out solos to some other soprano just because Trina had the misfortune not to be there at the time.

I told Trina that over my dead body was I going to allow her competitiveness with Karen Sue Walters to get in the way of my gastronomic choices at lunchtime, so we eat in the caf and not the choir room.

Luke had no way of knowing this, though. He looked over his shoulder at Karen Sue and the other people pulling their sack lunches out from beneath the risers as we left the choir room and went, "Isn't class over? Why are they eating in there?"

"Oh, you mean, what's with the land of misfit toys?" Trina laughed long and hard at her own joke, even though, given her druthers, she'd be right down there with them.

I was the one who had to explain. "They eat in there because they're scared."

"Scared of what?" Luke wanted to know.

Then we walked into the cafeteria.

And for the second time that day, Luke went, "Holy . . ."

Only this time it was for a different reason.

# Ask Annie

Dear Annie,

My boyfriend chews with his mouth open, and talks with it full of food. It's so embarrassing! I've mentioned it to him a million times, but he won't stop. How can I get him to have better manners?

Say It, Don't Spray It

Dear Spray It,

By refusing to sit at the same table with him until he learns to eat like a gentleman. A few meals on his lonesome, and he'll swallow before he speaks, guaranteed.

Annie

*Five*

*I suppose to* the uninitiated, the Clayton High School cafeteria might seem a little intimidating. I mean, you cram six hundred teenagers—we eat in two shifts—into any room, and it's going to be noisy.

But I guess Luke wasn't expecting the eardrum-splitting decibels of the din.

Then there's the fact that besides Glenwood Road—which is the main drag through downtown Clayton, up and down which people who have cars drive them every Saturday night—there is no other place that is more of a "scene" than the Clayton High School cafeteria. You can't just grab your food and go and sit down at a table and eat at Clayton High.

No, you have to walk down this long aisle of tables to get to where the food is sold—even if all you want is milk or a soda or whatever.

And while you walk down that aisle, every eye in the caf is on you. Seriously. It is in the caf that reputations are made or broken, depending on how cool you look as you walk up and down that aisle.

Unless, of course, you're me. Then, frankly, no one cares.

Luke, however, didn't know that. He stood in the doorway, staring in horror at the aisle, down which Courtney Deckard and some of her posse were sashaying.

"My God," he breathed. It was kind of hard to hear him above the noise. "It's worse than Sky Bar."

Trina piped up with, "We call it the catwalk. You ready to strut your stuff?"

Still looking stunned, Luke followed us as we made our way down the catwalk and toward the concession line. I didn't exactly notice the din lessen any as we went by, but I was definitely conscious that we'd managed to capture the attention of every female—from the tiniest freshman all the way to the most senior lunch lady—in the room.

Luke hardly seemed aware of the buzz he was creating. It was like he was in shock. When I handed him a tray, he took it wordlessly. When the lunch lady asked him if wanted corn or green beans, he seemed unable to make a choice. I told her corn, since it seemed to me that Luke, as a visitor to our state, might want to try the vegetable for which it is best known.

Once our trays were full, we made our way to the cash

register, where Luke was still apparently too stunned to fish out the two bucks his lunch cost. I paid. It's a good thing I'm such a popular baby-sitter—being boyfriendless, I am always available on Saturday night—because, otherwise, if I have to keep paying for Luke everywhere we go, I might go broke.

Trina and I put our trays down at the same table we'd been sitting at every day since freshman year—exactly in the middle of the room between the popular kids—the trendsetters—and the kids who weren't sensitive enough to have to eat in the choir room but weren't popular enough to sit with the jocks—the trendfollowers.

Trina and I aren't the only ones at the middle table. There's a bunch of other people who sit there, too. Those people include, but are not restricted to, by any means, most of the school's Merit scholars, brainiacs, computer geeks, drama freaks, punks, and the staff of the Clayton High *Register.*

Geri Lynn nearly choked on her flat Diet Coke as Luke Striker sat down in the chair beside hers and stared broodingly down at his food.

"Oh, hi," she said. "You must be Lucas."

See? See how fast word travels? I hadn't even seen Geri Lynn yet that day, and she'd already heard about the new guy. Could you imagine if word got out about my being Ask Annie? How short a time it would take to make it all the way around the school?

Luke didn't even look at Geri. Instead, he picked up his fork and stabbed at the food on his tray.

"What *is* this?" he wanted to know.

"Salisbury steak," I said. I myself had gotten pizza. I probably ought to have warned him to order off the concession line and not get the school lunch. But I'd figured that maybe, in his eagerness to experience everything midwestern, he'd want to try the steak.

"I'm a vegetarian," Luke said, mostly to the steak.

"They've got a salad bar," Trina, who wavers between ovo and lacto, depending on her mood, offered helpfully.

Scott had brought his own lunch, as he does every day. It's usually whatever he had cooked for dinner for himself and his dad the night before, neatly packed in Tupperware containers. Today's seemed to contain baked ziti and garlic bread, which Scott had heated up in the caf's microwave. It smelled really, really good.

"Are you going to eat that?" Scott asked Geri, in reference to the brownie in front of her.

"No, honey," Geri said, her gaze still locked on Luke. "You go ahead."

Scott picked up the brownie and took a bite. Then he made a face and set it down. The cafeteria staff's culinary skills are not equal to his own.

"You eat here every day?" Luke asked, closely examining a piece of Salisbury steak he'd skewered.

"It's a closed campus," I informed him. "Only seniors can leave school grounds at lunch. And even then, they only have Pizza Hut and McDonald's to choose from. Every other place is too far to make it back before sixth period."

Luke sighed and scraped the steak off his fork.

"You want some of this?" Scott asked, indicating what was left of his ziti. "It's got meat in it, but—"

Luke lowered his fork into Scott's Tupperware container without waiting for further invitation. He took a bite of ziti, chewed, and swallowed. As he did so, I could not help noticing that the gaze of every female in the vicinity—from Trina to Geri to the Japanese exchange student, Hisae—was riveted on his manly jaw.

"Man," Luke said, after swallowing. "That's good. Your mom make that or something?"

Scott isn't at all sensitive about the fact that he likes to cook. Unlike some guys, he would never think to deny that he knows how to make ziti. He didn't do so in front of "Lucas" either.

"Nah, I made it myself," he said. "Go ahead, finish it up. I'm gonna go get another soda."

Luke was scarfing down Scott's ziti with an enthusiasm surprising for one who professed not to eat meat, when all of a sudden, the cafeteria erupted in moos. Seriously. It was like we'd suddenly wandered into the 4-H tent at the Duane County Fair or something.

Luke spun around in his seat, trying to figure out what was going on. But all he saw was what the rest of us saw every single day, Cara Schlosburg making her way down the catwalk from the concession line.

Poor Cara. It's too bad she never made it into show choir. (She auditioned and everything, but didn't get in. Some of the snottier sopranos said it's because there aren't any bras padded enough to mimic Cara's chest and give us uniformity of appearance.) Because at least then she'd have had a safe place at lunchtime.

Instead, she tries to eat in the cafeteria like a normal person, and, frankly, that's never quite seemed to work out for her.

Cara's eyes, as they always did, filled up with tears as the mooing increased in volume the farther down the catwalk she got. She was holding a tray containing her usual low-cal lunch—a plate of lettuce, dressing on the side, a few breadsticks, and a diet soda.

But Kurt and his friends have no respect at all for the fact that Cara is trying, anyway, to lose weight. They just went on mooing, hardly even seeming aware they were doing it. I saw Courtney Deckard let out a moo, then go right back to her conversation with another cheerleader across the table from her, as if there hadn't even been an interruption.

"Shut up, you guys," Cara screamed at the side of the room where the popular kids sat, which was where most—though not all—of the mooing was coming from. "It's not funny!"

The saddest part of all is that I know Cara would have given anything in the world to be sitting there. You know, at the popular table with the mooers. Cara is one of those girls who worship the jocks and the cheerleaders, the popular people. I don't know why, because I've taken part in conversations with them, with Courtney Deckard or whoever, and they always go something like this: "Did you check out the sale at Bebe this weekend? Wasn't it the *best*?" or "I told them I wanted a French pedicure to show off my tan, but they made it way too pink, don't you think?"

Not, you know, that the conversations at my lunch table are more stimulating. But at least we talk about stuff besides what so-and-so was wearing at whoever's party, and whether or not the Tasti D-Lite at the Penguin really is fat-free.

But Cara's convinced she's missing out on something, so she tries and tries to get the popular people to accept her into their group, buying all the right clothes, wearing her hair the right way. . . .

But right for who? Not for Cara. Sure, she owned the exact same capris as Courtney Deckard. But she didn't look good in them—at least, not the way Courtney did in hers. Not even close.

And, sure, her hair was the same color as Courtney's, honey blond (courtesy of the same salon, even). But honey blond looks much better on girls like Courtney than it does on a girl like Cara.

Cara looked so bad, in fact, in the clothes and hairstyles that Courtney and her set insisted everyone needed to wear in order to be cool that the very people she was trying to impress could do nothing but smirk at her.

Or moo at her, actually.

It would have been one thing if she just hadn't cared what other people thought about her. I mean, there are lots of overweight people at Clayton. But the only one who ever gets any grief about it is Cara.

And Cara's reaction to the mooing just makes the mooing more fun for the mooers. People actually moo harder when Cara begs them to stop. I don't see why Cara doesn't see this. I've told her enough times . . . well, Ask Annie has, anyway.

But Cara can never do anything like a normal person. Instead of just taking her tray and going to sit down somewhere, out of the line of fire, Cara whirled around and around, trying to pinpoint exactly where the mooing was coming from.

"Stop it!" she shrieked. "I said, stop it!"

Finally, as inevitably happened most days, someone

threw a food item at Cara's head. This time it was a baked potato. It hit her square in the forehead, causing Cara to drop her tray—sending lettuce leaves and ranch dressing everywhere—and flee for the ladies' room, sobbing.

"Aw, geez," I said, because I knew this was my cue to get up and go try to comfort her.

"What the hell," Luke said, looking around, an indignant expression on his face, "is wrong with those people?"

"Oh, don't worry about Cara," Geri Lynn said. "Jen'll fix her up in time for the bell."

"Jen'll—" Luke looked at me like I was the visitor from the other planet, and not Cara. "This has happened before?"

Trina rolled her eyes. "Before? Every day, more like it."

I gave Luke a polite smile, then got up and headed after Cara.

I found Mr. Steele, the biology teacher who'd had the misfortune to pull lunchroom duty that day, standing just outside the ladies' room door, calling, "Cara, it's going to be all right. Why don't you just come out and tell me why you're so upset—"

As soon as he saw me, Mr. Steele's face crumpled with relief.

"Oh, Jenny," he said. "Thank God you're here. Could you make sure Cara's all right? I would, but, you know, it's the girls' room—"

"Sure thing, Mr. S.," I said.

"Thanks," he said. "You kids are the best."

I was kind of startled by the "you kids." I didn't realize, until I looked behind me, that I wasn't the only one from my table who'd exited the cafeteria. Luke was standing right behind me.

Thinking he was taking the whole shadowing me thing kind of seriously, I said, "Uh, I'll be out in a minute," and started to go inside after Cara.

But to my surprise, Luke took me by the arm and, dragging me out of earshot of Mr. Steele, went, "What *was* that back there?"

"What was what?" I really didn't know what he was talking about.

"*That* back there. That mooing thing." Luke actually looked a little upset. Well, maybe *upset* is too strong a word for it. What he looked was annoyed. "You know, when I volunteered for this thing, I didn't exactly expect it to be like the schoolroom on *Little House on the Prairie*. But I didn't think it would be like a cell block in some prison drama."

I am no fan of Clayton High School—or any high school, really, except maybe that one for the performing arts, the one in *Fame*, where everybody danced on taxicabs in the street—but I still couldn't understand how Luke could compare it to jail. Clayton High is nothing like jail. For one thing, there are no bars on the windows.

And for another, prisoners get reduced sentences for good behavior. The only thing you get in high school for not killing each other is a diploma that is good for exactly nothing, except possibly a managerial position at Rax Roast Beef.

"Um," I said. "I'm sorry." What was he talking about? Why was he so upset? I mean, yeah, it's mean how they treat Cara, but what am *I* supposed to do about it? "But I sort of have to go—"

"No," Luke said, his blue eyes still burning like pieces of kryptonite behind the lenses of his glasses. "I want to know. I want to know why you didn't try to stop those people from tormenting that poor girl."

"Look," I said. Cara's wails were getting louder, and I knew the bell was going to ring any minute.

But I don't know. Something came over me. Maybe it was the stress of having a movie star in disguise following me around all day. Or maybe it was residual tension from being yelled at for an hour by Mr. Hall about my jazz hands.

In any case, I think I sort of snapped. I mean, where did he get off, basically saying nothing at all to me for most of the day, then turning around and yelling at *me* about something Kurt Schraeder and his friends were doing?

"If you disapprove of this place so much," I hissed, "why

don't you just go back to Hollywood? I wouldn't mind, you know, because I actually have more important things to do than baby-sit prima donnas like you."

Then I turned around and went into the ladies' room.

I'll admit that, even though my speech sounded cool and all, I wasn't feeling very cool. In fact, my heart was beating kind of fast, and I felt a little bit like hurling my pizza. Because really, I don't yell at people. Ever.

And the fact that I'd yelled at this very famous movie star whom I had been assigned to be nice to by the principal and Juicy Lucy . . . well, I was kind of scared. Scared that Luke would tell Dr. Lewis what I'd said. Scared that I'd consequently get expelled. And scared that I wouldn't get that diploma after all and have to work as a drill press operator, just like I'd put on my state achievement test.

Only I'd been joking! I don't want to be a drill press operator! I mean, I'm excellent at solving other people's problems . . . and you know, layout and all of that. I can see how things fit together and what should go where, which is why I'm not only Ask Annie but I help out a lot with set design for the Drama Club. I want to be a therapist—or a designer or both—when I'm grown-up. Not a drill press operator.

Except that it's kind of hard to be a therapist *or* a designer on an eleventh grade education.

But I didn't really have time to worry about Luke just then. Because I still had Cara to deal with.

"Cara," I said, going to lean against the stall door she'd locked herself behind. "Come out. It's me, Jen."

"Why?" Cara sobbed. "Why do they keep doing that me, Jen?"

"Because they're idiots. Now come on out."

Cara came out. Her face was blotchy with tears. If she didn't spend so much time crying, and stopped trying to blow-dry her hair so it was stick straight like Courtney Deckard's and just let it curl on its own the way it wanted to, and knocked off the capris, which don't look that good on someone her shape, I suspect she might even have been pretty.

"It's not fair," Cara said, sniffling. "I try and I try . . . I even told them my parents were going out of town last weekend and that they could use my house to party in. Did anybody show up? No."

I turned on the water in one of the sinks and wet a paper towel to wipe the potato guts out of Cara's hair.

"I've told you before," I said. "They're idiots, Cara."

"They aren't idiots. They rule the school. How can the people who rule the school be idiots?" She looked woefully at her reflection in the glass above the sinks. "It's me. It's just me. I'm such a loser."

"You're not a loser, Cara," I said. "And they don't rule the school. The student council does, technically."

"But they're still *popular*," Cara pointed out.

"There are more important things than being popular, Cara."

"That's easy for you to say, Jen," Cara said. "I mean, everybody likes you. EVERYBODY. You've never had people mooing at you."

This is true. But I also never went out of my way to try to *get* people to like me the way Cara does.

When I mentioned this, though, Cara just went, "You sound just like Ask Annie. *Be yourself.* That's what she's always saying."

"It's good advice," I said.

"Sure," Cara said sadly. "If you know who yourself even is."

The bell rang, long and loud. A second later, the ladies' room was filled with girls eager to check their hair before heading off to class. My tête-à-tête with Cara was at an end. For now.

"I'll see you later," I said to her. She just sniffled in reply and dug around in her purse for some tissue. I wasn't surprised. Cara never thanked me for coming to check on her after one of her spaz attacks. It was one of the reasons, I was pretty sure, why she has no real friends. She just doesn't know how to treat people.

I have to admit that, what with the whole Cara thing, I'd kind of forgotten about Luke Striker . . . at least until I came out of the ladies' room and there he was, waiting for me.

The sick feeling came right back to my stomach. What was he still doing there? I'd really thought that, after my outburst, he'd have stalked off and called his limo to come pick him up. Instead, he came up to me and, hands in his pockets, asked, "So what do we have next?"

Just like that. Like nothing had happened. Like I hadn't told him to go back to Hollywood or anything.

What did this mean? That he wasn't going running to Dr. Lewis, to tell him what I'd said? Was he just going to pretend my meltdown hadn't happened? What kind of person *does* that? I am very good at figuring people out. Except, apparently, Luke Striker.

The knot in my stomach loosened a little after this, but I still didn't feel completely at ease. I didn't know what had caused Luke to change his mind about me and Clayton High—or even *if* he'd changed his mind—but I did know one thing:

I doubted either of us was going to be able to live up to his expectations.

# Ask Annie

Ask Annie your most complex interpersonal relationship questions. Go on, we dare you! All letters to Annie are subject to publication in the Clayton High School *Register*. Names and e-mail addresses of correspondents guaranteed confidential.

Dear Annie,

My girlfriend won't stop giving me hickeys. It's embarrassing. I'm glad she loves me and all, but . . . ew. Why won't she stop and what can I do to make her?

Tired of Wearing Turtlenecks

Dear Turtleneck,

Your girlfriend is giving you hickeys because she wants everyone to know you're taken. Tell her to knock it off, or you'll find a girl who isn't as insecure.

Annie

*I should have* known everybody in school was going to fall in love with Luke. I mean, even in his Lucas Smith guise, he's still totally cute. And, face it, any guy who isn't completely obsessed with monster trucks or doesn't wear a mullet can be considered hot at Clayton High.

Luke was neither of those things, AND over six feet tall, AND sensitive enough to think the way everyone treated Cara was lame, AND he looked just like . . . well, Luke Striker.

Hey, it was a wonder *I* hadn't fallen in love with him. I guess I shouldn't have blamed Trina for it. Falling for the new guy, I mean.

It's not like I didn't suspect it might happen. Trina loves Luke Striker more than she loves her cat, Mr. Momo, and Mr. Momo's been Trina's constant companion since the second grade.

Still, I didn't realize what was going on until I was in Steve's car on the way home. Neither Trina nor I have our drivers' licenses yet, because

a) our parents are afraid to teach us and they don't offer drivers ed. in our school and,
b) even if they did, there's nowhere worth driving to in Clayton and
c) even if there were, we always have Trina's boyfriend, Steve, who does have a car, to drive us there.

Fortunately for me, Trina and Steve always stay late at school, rehearsing for whatever play the Drama Club is doing. Right now it's this major yawn called *Spoon River Anthology*, which happens to be about dead people—but not zombies or anything cool—just dead people sitting around in a graveyard talking about what it had been like to be alive, I guess to make us all appreciate our loved ones more or something. I'd told Trina I'd go to opening night and all, but I fully plan to sit in the back row with the latest Dean Koontz and a book light.

I probably could have gotten a ride home with Scott—he always remembers to ask if I need one.

But lately catching rides with Scott hasn't been all that

much fun, on account of Geri Lynn's moodiness. I mean, I'll be sitting in the backseat, having a perfectly civil conversation with Scott about something or other—like *The Two Towers* and how I thought the ents looked kind of Jar Jar Binks-ish or whatever, a fact he strenuously denies—and suddenly Geri Lynn will interrupt with something like this:

*Geri Lynn: Scott, did you remember to ask Ellis Floral if they were running their annual Spring Fling special clip 'n' save coupon on corsages?*

And then the conversation goes from ents and Jar Jar Binks to this:

*Scott: No, Geri, I didn't ask Ellis Floral if they were running their annual Spring Fling special clip 'n' save coupon on corsages because that's Charlene's job. She's in charge of ad placements.*

*Geri Lynn: Scott, your duty as editor in chief is to oversee all* aspects *of the paper. You can't expect Charlene, who is a freshman and wasn't even at Clayton last year for the Spring Fling, to remember to ask Ellis Floral if they're running another special.*

*Me: Um, actually, Geri, I noticed their ad didn't have the coupon when I was laying that page out, so I called them and they are, so I put it in.*

*Geri Lynn: Well, it's good to know* someone *on staff is paying attention.*

See? Talk about uncomfortable. It's just easier to get a ride with Steve.

As Luke and I emerged from our session at the *Register*—yeah, he even came to my after-school meeting at the paper. How interesting could *that* have been for him? Although he and Geri Lynn did get into a pretty spirited argument about a celebrity's right to privacy, with Geri insisting that journalists play an important part in building up a celebrity's status and that anybody who willingly takes on a job in the public eye should expect to be stalked by paparazzi and Luke, not surprisingly, having a different view of things. Luke went, "So that was a typical day in your life?"

"Yeah," I said. "I guess so."

It was kind of weird to think about—you know, your life from somebody else's perspective. Especially somebody who has such a *different* sort of life from mine. I mean, my life must seem really, really boring to Luke, compared to his own, which I'm sure is filled with invitations to club openings, stints on talk shows, movie premieres, nude scenes, chocolate body paint, and that sort of thing.

But Luke didn't say anything about it. I mean, about how boring my life is compared to his. Instead, he said, "Okay, then."

*Okay, then?* What did *that* mean? What was *up* with this guy? Why couldn't I figure out what made him tick? I mean, that's what I *do*.

It was right at that moment that Steve pulled up in his Chevette, and Trina leaned out and was all, "Going our way?"

Which of course I fully was. But it turned out Luke had other plans.

"Sorry," he said. "I'm meeting someone."

Of course it was totally ridiculous that the new guy should be "meeting someone" at five o'clock in front of the Clayton High flagpole his very first day there. But neither Trina nor Steve seemed to think anything about it. They just went, "Okay, bye," and, after I'd piled into the car, drove away.

Neither of them, of course, turned in their seat and looked back. Because if they had, they would have seen a big black limo pull up into the turnaround a few seconds after we'd pulled away and Luke high-five whoever was inside it before climbing in himself.

All I could think was, *Where did he get that limo?* Because there is no limo company in Clayton. Our town is too small to support one, since the only time people here ever need one is at the Spring Fling.

Anyway, that was when Trina started talking about Luke. Or Lucas, I should say. She talked about him all the way home, and then, after dinner, when I went upstairs to do my homework, she e-mailed me about him.

All she could talk about was Lucas this and Lucas that. Did I think Lucas had liked his first day at Clayton High? Did I know why his parents had decided to move so late in the school year? Why hadn't he stayed at his old school? He could only have had a few months to go before graduation. Wasn't he going to miss graduating with his old friends? Did he like living out by the lake? Did he have a girlfriend at his old school? Did I think it was serious?

And the clincher, the one I'd been dreading all day:

Didn't I think Lucas looked uncannily like Luke Striker?

I tried to answer Trina's questions as best I could without outright lying, but of course it was hard. I mean, I *had* to lie for a few of them. It was turning out to be no joke, student guiding a movie star. You know, really, Mr. Mitchell should be *paying* me for letting Luke follow me around. There was a lot of work involved. . . .

Not the least of which was the abuse I'd had to put up

with from Luke himself. That night, as I lay in bed, looking up at my canopy—I had been nuts for princesses as a kid and had begged and begged for a princess bed, so my mom, being an interior decorator and all, had gotten me the most princessy bed available in southern Indiana, and now I was fully stuck with it—I thought about what Luke had said to me outside the caf about Cara.

Luke hadn't known what he was talking about, of course. I mean, he didn't know the effort I'd put into being nice to Cara, all the times I'd run after her into the bathroom, all the tears I'd mopped up, all the advice I'd given her (none of which she'd taken). He didn't know about my being Ask Annie and all the letters from Cara I'd answered. He didn't know how much worse it might actually have been for Cara if I hadn't been around.

And he *really* didn't know what it was like to be me. It was exhausting, frankly. Between Cara and the Ask Annie thing and the Trina and Steve thing and the kidnapping of Betty Ann and the arm movements in Troubadours . . .

It's a wonder I even get up in the morning, really.

I have to admit, I didn't really expect to see Luke the next day. I mean, after all the problems he'd had waking up the day before, the lack of espresso on school grounds, the Salisbury steak—not to mention the whole Cara thing—I figured he'd probably had enough. He might have been dedicated to his craft and all, but who would put up with conditions like those? Especially a millionaire.

So when he walked into Latin the next morning, I nearly choked. He had abandoned the football jersey for something that looked like it had been woven out of one of those Mexican blankets, open at the chest to reveal one of those pooka shell necklaces surfers always wear. He'd ditched the cross trainers, too, in favor of suede Pumas.

Plus he'd managed to find some espresso . . . or at least a latte grande, in a tall paper cup. He looked a thousand times more awake than he had the day before.

"Hey, Jen," he said, sliding into the seat behind me.

I have to admit, I was shocked to see him. What was he *doing* here? I'd been sure that he wouldn't be coming back. Sure of it.

Only now he was back. He hadn't disappeared after all.

I turned around and whispered, glad the second bell hadn't rung yet so there weren't a lot of people in the room, "What are you *doing* here?"

Luke blinked at me from behind the wire-rimmed glasses. "What do you mean? I'm staying for two weeks. Didn't they tell you?"

"Um, yeah," I whispered, "but I just . . . I just figured. . . ."

"I was a quick study?" Luke smiled. It was the same

smile that had melted hearts all over the world when he'd flashed it at Angelique Tremaine's Guenevere. And, I'll admit, it gave me a flutter.

But not enough of one not to be all, "Luke—"

"Lucas," he corrected me.

"Lucas, then. You . . . I mean, you so obviously hated it here." And then, because I felt I had to, I added, "Hated me, too."

The smile disappeared. "What are you talking about, Jen? I don't hate you."

"But the whole Cara thing—"

"Well, yeah," he said with a grimace. "That wasn't too pleasant. But after you yelled at me, I got . . . curious."

"Curious? About what?" Then I added hastily, "And I never yelled at you. I was just—"

"Letting off steam. I know. Still." He opened the latte and released its rich aroma into the air. "I want to see how it all turns out."

I stared at him like he was nuts. "How *what* turns out?" I asked him. "What are you talking about?"

But I never found out, because just then the bell rang.

I wouldn't say that, after that moment, Luke and I started getting along like—well, like Lancelot and Guenevere or anything. I mean, he still walked around with this little frown on his face a lot of the time . . . especially when there wasn't anything worth frowning over going on at all. Like when Courtney Deckard and her friends walked by us in the hall, they'd all lower their gazes to Luke's feet, then slowly lift them along the length of his body, until they met his eyes. Then they'd smile.

Why should *this* make him frown? That's how the popular crowd communicates. Everyone knows this. They are checking out his outfit to make sure it's regulation trendy. This is status quo for the popular set.

Other times, he seemed to find stuff that wasn't funny at all totally hilarious. Like during show choir rehearsal. Luke seemed to find Mr. Hall's constant nagging of me to "quit sloughing off" and get Trina her hat faster during "All That Jazz" absolutely thigh-slappingly funny.

Although I honestly don't know what cracked him up so much about that. It's no joke, trying to get from the top of the riser down to the bottom in time for the sopranos can-can, or whatever it was. I finally figured out that if I threw Trina the hat from the top of the riser, she could get it in time to join the kick line with Karen Sue Walters and all those guys.

I'm not the world's best thrower, but Trina is an excellent catcher, so that seemed to work. At least, Mr. Hall quit yelling at me and moved on to yell at the baritones.

I guess after his initial shock at the barbarism existing in a modern-day high school, Luke mellowed out a little. Even lunch seemed not to faze him. It helped that the second day, he brought his own. Of course, that nearly blew his cover—or at least I thought so—since the lunch he brought had so obviously been flown in from Indianapolis. I mean, there are no sushi places in Clayton. We don't even have a limo company! How are we going to have sushi?

But Luke—pretty smoothly, I thought—explained that he'd made the sushi himself, with tuna from the fish counter at Mr. D's. I have to admit, this almost made me choke on my Diet Coke. But Luke said it so matter-of-factly that even Scott believed him. In fact, the two of them got into this whole conversation about sushi-grade tuna and flash freezing. I had no idea what they were talking about, but I was pleased that my friends were making an effort to make the new guy feel welcome. . . .

Until I remembered Luke wasn't actually "the new guy." He was the former star of *Heaven Help Us*, ex-boyfriend of Angelique Tremaine, a breathtaking Tarzan in his loincloth, and a heroic and tragic Lancelot. It was a testament to Luke's acting skills, I suppose, that even *I* began to think of him as Lucas Smith, transfer student. He didn't break out of the character of Lucas at all that next day—

Except for once. And that was right after first period, when he learned of the kidnapping of Betty Ann Mulvaney.

"Why are you taking Latin?" Luke asked me as we moved toward my locker after class. "I mean, isn't it a dead language? Nobody even speaks it anymore."

"It's good to know," I said, using the standard response I give everyone. Because the truth is too weird to explain. "For the SATs."

"You don't need it," Luke said with kind of an alarming amount of confidence for someone who'd only met me twenty-four hours ago. "You work for the school paper. You know all about grammar and stuff. What are you *really* taking it for?"

Maybe because he's older—only nineteen, but much older than most nineteen-year-olds, considering he has his own house in the Hollywood Hills and that his paychecks are about ten million dollars more than what my dad makes every year, not to mention his commitment tattoo and all— I told him the truth.

"I heard Mrs. Mulvaney was a really good teacher," I whispered in case Courtney Deckard or any of her friends might be around, listening. "So I signed up for her class."

Luke understood even better than I thought he would.

"Oh, yeah," he said. "That's like in acting. If you want to work with a really good director, you take the part, no matter what it is or what the movie's about. Only . . . well, no offense, but Mrs. M. doesn't seem all that great. I mean, she just kind of seems to . . . be there."

"Oh," I said. "Yeah. Well, right *now*. She's a little off these days, on account of Betty Ann."

Luke asked who Betty Ann was, and I told him. I guess I told him a little too much—like the rumor about how Mrs. Mulvaney hadn't been able to have kids and that Betty Ann was her substitute baby, in a way. The truth was, I was still worried. About what Kurt and those guys were going to do to Betty Ann. Because I didn't think any of them were smart enough to realize how important Betty Ann was to Mrs. Mulvaney. I mean, to Mrs. M., Betty Ann isn't just a doll or the school mascot or anything. She's kind of like . . . well, family.

Telling Luke that was a mistake, though.

"Kidnapped her?" he practically yelled, right there in the hallway. "What for?"

"It's a prank," I explained. "The senior prank."

"Oh, yeah, very funny," he said. "When are they going to give her back?"

"Well, after graduation, I guess," I said. I hoped.

But that wasn't a good enough answer.

"*After* graduation?" Luke was appalled. "Do you know who did it? Who has her?"

"Well," I said. "Yeah."

"So make them give her back," Luke said. "Make them

do some other prank. This one's not funny."

I agreed with him, of course, but what could I do? I was just a lowly junior. I had no control over Kurt and his friends.

Only it turned out Luke didn't quite see it that way.

"That's not true," Luke said to me. "And you know it, Jen."

I told Luke what I'd said to Kurt that day—the day he'd first stuffed Betty Ann into his backpack. I told Luke how I'd asked Kurt what he was doing. And that Kurt had told me to relax.

Luke, hearing this, just shook his head. He didn't say anything more about it after that.

But I noticed that he was especially nice to Mrs. Mulvaney. Luke was nice to everyone—which was why practically every girl in school, not just Trina, had fallen in love with him before the weekend even rolled around—but he was more than nice to Mrs. Mulvaney, bringing along a latte grande for her, too, every morning, holding the door open for her, and even taking stabs at some conjugations.

In fact, if anything seemed to cheer up Mrs. Mulvaney—the spread in the *Register* wasn't enough to get the perpetrators to step forward, and Kurt's ransom note, which said only *Give all the seniors As for the semester, or Betty Ann bites it,* seemed hardly in the fun-loving spirit a senior prank should be—it was Luke. Mrs. M. seemed totally enamored of him, to the point that about the only time she smiled anymore was when he walked into the room.

Mrs. Mulvaney, like I mentioned, was hardly the only one who lacked immunity to Luke's charms. Trina was falling harder for him every day. She came right out and asked him for his cell phone number—in front of poor Steve, no less, who looked crushed but didn't say a word about it—and then complained bitterly to me when she called and only got Luke's voice mail. Eleven times.

But Trina didn't seem suspicious. If anything, Luke's very unavailability seemed to make him *more* appealing.

The same was true of Geri Lynn. She couldn't seem to get enough of Luke . . . especially at lunch and at *Register* meetings. Which was especially weird since all the two of them ever seemed to do was argue. Geri Lynn was always going on about the vital role journalists play in the making or breaking of a celebrity's career, while Luke made no effort to hide his opinion that journalists are muckraking backstabbers only out to make a buck. The bickering finally got to the point where Scott assigned them a pro and con column, Geri Lynn taking the pro-paparazzi stance, and Luke the con.

I have to admit Luke's column was surprisingly well written. Which only deepened my confusion about him. Sometimes he seemed totally bored and uninterested in everything and everyone at Clayton High. But at other times (like over the whole Cara thing) he got surprisingly serious and intense. This guy was clearly smart, too.

But while I could forgive Trina for her crush on Luke, I couldn't quite bring myself to be so sanguine about Geri Lynn—who, in spite of the fact that she seemed to argue with him nonstop, nevertheless couldn't take her eyes off him whenever he was in the room. I mean, it's not like Geri was going out with Steve, who isn't exactly the world's hottest guy. She was going out with Scott Bennett . . . who I know most people wouldn't consider anything but a geek of the first order, being, you know, the editor of the school paper and a lover of reading and cooking.

But those people don't know Scott. They'd never argued with him, as I had, over the merits of the reissue of Stephen King's *The Stand*, with the edited bits put back in.

They had never tasted, as I had, his cold cucumber soup.

They had never, as I had, listened at a campfire as he described his parents' painful breakup; his decision to go and live with his mom; and then, years later, his decision to come back to Clayton and give living with his dad another try.

They had never noticed, as I had, that Scott's eyes are even more hazel than mine, sometimes looking green and sometimes even amber, the same color as the stuff the mosquitos were stuck in in *Jurassic Park*.

They had never watched Scott's strong capable hands move over a computer keyboard as he corrected my Ask Annie copy. Or lift them up to grab a log before a wall of peanut butter crashed down on them.

They had never heard the butternut squash story.

Was a mere movie star worth throwing a guy like that away for?

Even if that movie star blew his cover, and everyone in the whole world suddenly knew that he wasn't a transfer student at all, and *Entertainment Tonight* and *People* magazine started knocking on your door?

Even if that movie star happened to ask you to the Spring Fling?

# Ask Annie

Ask Annie your most complex interpersonal relationship questions. Go on, we dare you! All letters to Annie are subject to publication in the Clayton High School *Register*. Names and e-mail addresses of correspondents guaranteed confidential.

Dear Annie,
I think my boyfriend is cheating on me, but he denies it. How can I tell whether or not he's lying?
  Dating a Dog

Dear Dating,
If he's cheating, he'll be exhibiting at least a few of the following behaviors:

• He is spending more and more Saturday nights "with the guys."
• He gets cell phone calls while he's with you that he doesn't answer after checking the caller ID.
• He suddenly starts caring about his hair/wardrobe.
• He accuses YOU of cheating on HIM (guilt).

- He asks weird, seemingly random questions like, "Do you think it's possible to love two people at the same time?"
- He gets a new job or has to "work" all the time.
- He shows a sudden interest in a type of music or band he's never liked before.
- He stops e-mailing you as much as he used to, but seems to spend more time online.
- He gets a new e-mail address.
- He stops trying to get into your pants.

Most important of all, if you suspect he might be cheating, he probably is . . . trust your gut. Unless you're one of those stupid, insecure girls who always thinks her boyfriend is cheating on her even when he isn't—in which case, get a grip.

Annie

*Seven*

*It started, the* way these kinds of things always seem to, innocently enough. We were at the car wash on Saturday morning—the one the Troubadours were holding, to raise money for our stupid dresses for the stupid show choir invitational the following week.

It's kind of iffy scheduling a car wash during an Indiana spring, because you just never know what you're going to get, weatherwise. I mean, after June 1, you can pretty much be assured of warm weather. But you also run the risk of the occasional thunderstorm and even a tornado now and then. But mostly those hold off until later in June.

Still, you never knew if you'd wake up on any given Saturday in June and have a perfect spring day—temperatures in the seventies, warm breezes blowing the scent of honeysuckle everywhere, clear blue sky, rustling green leaves in the treetops—or something gray and blustery, with temps in the sixties and your toes freezing in the sandals you wore so comfortably the day before.

The Saturday of the Troubadour car wash, though, was like summer. By ten in the morning, it was eighty. Trina called and was all, "I'm wearing my swimsuit and cutoffs. You better, too."

I obliged her but only to get her off my back about Luke. She'd been pestering me since the night before about whether or not I thought he'd be showing up at the car wash. The truth was, I needed a day off from Luke. I mean, he's nice and all—and of course extremely easy on the eyes—but a girl can only put up with so much. By the time Steve and Trina dropped me off at home Friday night, my nerves were shot. Between trying to

a) keep people from finding out that Lucas Smith was really Luke Striker and not a transfer student after all and

b) prevent Luke from thinking everyone at Clayton High was devil spawn on account of the whole Betty Ann and Cara Cow thing and

c) get Trina her hat on time during "All That Jazz," let alone learn the choreography and

d) not slack off all my other stuff, like Ask Annie and trig and keeping Cara from killing herself and all of that,

I was a wreck.

It was a relief to go baby-sit that night. I actually enjoyed playing Candyland seven million times in a row.

I wasn't looking forward to the car wash. Trina and I usually spend at least part of our Saturdays at the mall, where we inevitably run into people we know, like Geri Lynn and Scott, for instance, at the Barnes & Noble, where we invariably fall into a long conversation about what's new in the sci-fi aisle. Scott and I do, I mean. Geri Lynn and Trina usually go off and look at magazines.

Plus, I mean, hanging out with my fellow Troubadours isn't exactly a thrill. Don't get me wrong, I love the altos. Too-tall Kim and Pudgy Deb and Shy Audrey and Tough Brenda and Bored Liz are my homegirls. We have totally bonded over the la-la-las on middle C.

But the other misfit toys, as Trina had called them (though not, I noticed, until after she'd convinced me to join them) can get kind of annoying—especially the sopranos. They all totally worship Mr. Hall and will do anything he says . . . kind of like those clones in *Star Wars II*.

And the tenors can be a little irritating, too. Most of them are freshmen or sophomores, and you know freshmen and sophomore boys. It's all about fart jokes and Limp Bizkit. Even with guys who'd willingly sign up to be in a choir.

But it wasn't like I had much of a choice. Thanks to Trina.

And I'd only have to put up with being a Troubadour for a couple more weeks, and then school would be out. It didn't matter what kind of pressure Trina put on me either: No way was I auditioning again next year.

Anyway, even though there were a lot of places I'd rather have been than the Troubadours' car wash—playing Candyland with some four-year-olds comes to mind—it helped that the weather was so nice. Trina and I really would be able to work on our tans—with the help of SPF 30, since, being the girl-next-door type, I burn more than I tan. So it wasn't a total loss.

At least that's what I figured at the time.

Because Mr. Hall wanted to raise as much money as possible—some girls didn't have a hundred and eighty dollars to blow on a dress, even one with a sequined lightning bolt down the front, I guess because some girls don't baby-sit as much as I do—he'd asked the Chi-Chi's Mexican restaurant on the corner right before you pull into the mall if we could have our car wash in their parking lot, and Chi-Chi's, for community-relations reasons I suppose, said yes.

So when Steve and Trina and I showed up for our twelve-to-two shift at the car wash, there was actually quite a bit of action going on. Besides all the cars belonging to the friends and parents of members of the Troubadours—and there are thirty of us, so you know that's a lot of cars—there were the cars belonging to the people who'd showed up to have lunch at Chi-Chi's, the cars belonging to the people who worked at Chi-Chi's, as well as the cars belonging to all the people who couldn't figure out anything better to do on a beautiful Saturday than go to the mall.

In all, a lot of cars.

Business was jumping. We'd been in the parking lot for maybe two seconds before Mr. Hall came racing up, a bucket of soapy water and a sponge for each of us, and went, "Get to work! We've raised two hundred dollars in just the past two hours. But we need two thousand more before we can knock off for the day."

I don't want to cast Clayton in a bad light or anything— I mean, except for the occasional bias crime (it's southern Indiana, after all), it's a pretty nice place to live.

But can I just say that the Troubadour car wash wouldn't be making half the money it was if it weren't for the fact that Karen Sue and a bunch of the other sopranos were standing out by the Chi-Chi's sign, wearing nothing but bikinis?

And, okay, they were holding signs that said SUPPORT CLAYTON HIGH'S TROUBADOURS, but I highly doubt that's why so many guys in pickups, who were clearly on their way to go fishing up at Clayton Lake or whatever, pulled in.

You have to have pretty big . . . um, lungs, to be a soprano. Well, at least if you're a Clayton High Troubadour. Thus, you know, the padded bras Mr. Hall has us wear for "uniformity of appearance."

Anyway, Trina and Steve and I grabbed our sponges and buckets and went to work. I found my fellow altos, and we were having a pretty good time cleaning people's station wagons and occasionally flicking soap suds at one another, when all of a sudden, out of the corner of my eye, I saw Scott Bennett's beat-up old Audi. He and Geri Lynn had been going by on their way to the mall, spotted us, and pulled over to join in the fun.

Well, at least Scott wanted to join in the fun. He even forked over ten bucks for us to wash his car.

Geri Lynn didn't look as if she was very thrilled with the idea, though. Apparently, they'd been on their way to Compusave, to look at laptops. Scott was going to help Geri pick one out for college.

"Compusave's not going anywhere, Ger," Scott said to Geri Lynn, when she objected to stopping.

Then, even though he'd paid us to do it, he picked up a sponge and started helping us wash his car. In fact, he started scrubbing right next to where I was working on one of his hubcaps.

Geri, in a yellow mini and espadrilles, wasn't really dressed to help wash a car, though, so she kind of flounced over to where the sopranos were standing by the Chi-Chi's sign and started talking to Karen Sue Walters about the Spring Fling. Geri and Scott were going, of course. Karen Sue was going with one of the tenors. I guess she and Geri have a lot in common, seeing as how they're both dating younger men.

"So I finished *Lucifer's Hammer*," Scott said to me, as I was picking dried-up mud out of his hubcap.

I'd forgotten I'd loaned him that one. We both have a fixation on books that feature huge disasters that threaten the destruction of Earth as we know it.

"Oh yeah?" I said. "What'd you think of it?"

"I thought it was a load of right-wing bull," Scott said.

And then we were off. Trina even went, "There they go" and rolled her eyes, because she'd heard Scott and me arguing over a book before.

And it probably isn't the best way to get a guy to like you. I mean, by telling him that his views on a book are all wrong. But the fact is, with Scott I have nothing to lose, since he obviously doesn't like me that way, seeing as how he's attached at the hip to Geri Lynn.

So we had a good time arguing over *Lucifer's Hammer*, which is a science fiction novel about a giant comet that hits Earth and destroys huge sections of it and how the people who survive have to decide who gets access to what limited food is left. The book raises interesting philosophical questions, like who is more important in building a new society, a doctor or an artist? A lawyer or a convict? Who do you let live, and who do you let die?

I insisted that *Lucifer's Hammer* was a survival story about the worth of the individual. Scott said it was political commentary on the socioeconomics of the seventies. Trina and Steve, who hadn't read the book, stayed out of it and just groaned whenever one of us said a word like *facile* or *specious*.

But arguing with Scott about books is seriously fun.

At least until Scott looked at me and went, "You're getting more water on yourself than on the car. "

Which was true. Washing cars, it turns out, requires the same amount of physical coordination as dancing. And while I might be able to settle arguments between people with ease, physical coordination is not apparently something I have in abundance.

I don't know what came over me. I really don't. It was like for a second I was seized by the soul of some other girl, some flirty girl like Trina or Geri Lynn. All I know is, a second later I went, "Oh, yeah?" and threw my sponge at Scott, hitting him square in the center of his chest. "Well, welcome to the club."

Next thing I knew, Scott was chasing me around the parking lot, threatening to dump a bucket of soapy water over my head if he caught me. Everyone stopped what they were doing to laugh . . . everybody except Geri Lynn, that is.

She came stomping over to us, looking pretty peeved.

"Look at you," she said to Scott. "You're soaked!"

Scott looked down at himself. "It's just water, Ger," he said.

"But we can't go to the mall with you looking like that," she said, stamping one of her espadrilled feet. "You're all wet!"

"It'll dry," Scott said. By that time, we were done with his car, so he handed the bucket of water back to me. I was kind of disappointed he hadn't poured it over my head like he'd been threatening to. Don't ask me why.

"Not for hours!" Geri cried.

"Aw, come on, Geri," I said. "We were just goofing around. And besides, nobody at Compusave will care."

"I care," Geri Lynn said, actually looking tearful. "I care. Don't *I* count?"

That's when I knew this wasn't about a wet T-shirt. It also wasn't something that I could fix. This had to do with Geri's insecurities over leaving for college, Scott's still having a year left of high school, and probably, though I didn't know for sure, those little hearts in Geri's date book.

Realizing this, I turned around and went over to where Trina and Steve and the altos were, snagged a new sponge and got very busy on the sedan they were cleaning.

"Looks like trouble in paradise," Trina sang, shooting a

look over her shoulder at Geri and Scott, who were standing on the edge of the parking lot by his car, speaking very earnestly—but unfortunately inaudibly, at least to us—to each other.

"I never thought they made a very good couple," Bored Liz said. "Geri's too needy. And what's with all the flat Diet Coke?"

"Hey, now," I said, because I felt guilty. I knew their fight wasn't my fault, exactly, but I shouldn't have thrown that sponge at him. Loaning another girl's boyfriend books is one thing. I mean, after all, Scott and I are friends. But throwing a wet sponge at him? That's not as forgivable. "Geri's nice."

"What she's gonna be is single," Tough Brenda declared, "if she don't watch herself. You can only push a boy like that so far."

"Yeah," Trina muttered in a voice audible only to me, "but if they break up, then he'll be free, and you can finally ask him out, Jen, the way I told you to way back at the beginning of the year."

"Trina!" I was shocked. I mean, poor Geri! Poor Scott!

Mr. Hall, who was the one collecting all the money, came over just then and clapped his hands.

"That's enough chitchat!" he said, his goatee all atremble. "Work, people! Work!"

It was right then that Luke appeared, seemingly from nowhere. I mean, I hadn't seen his limo anywhere.

"Luke!" I couldn't help crying out when I saw him. Then I added, hastily, "Us. I mean, Lucas."

"Hey," Luke said, grinning in a kind of lopsided way as he strolled up to us through the parking lot. Unlike the rest of us, Luke wasn't wearing a swimsuit and shorts. He was fully dressed in jeans and a flannel shirt. It seemed a little warm for flannel, but maybe that's what Luke thought a high school boy would wear to a car wash. "Sorry I'm late."

"Wow, you came," Trina cried, bouncing up to him. "That's so great! Jen wasn't sure you'd be able to make it."

The truth was, Luke and I had never discussed his weekend plans. I'd just figured he'd stay at his condo at the lake and show up at school on Monday. It had never occurred to me he might . . . well, want to hang out with a bunch of high school kids instead. I felt a little guilty for not asking if he'd like to join us.

But Luke obviously had needed no invitation.

"Change of plans," Luke said, still grinning easily at Trina. "Besides, looks like you guys need all the help you can get. You got a line of cars all the way back to Rax."

Trina ran and got Luke a bucket and sponge, and soon, right before my disbelieving eyes, he started washing away right there with us, laughing and joking and having what looked to me like a genuinely good time. Everybody was. Having a good time, I mean.

Everybody but Scott and Geri, that is. They were still arguing down at the other end of the parking lot. I was trying not to stare and all—also trying not to tell myself that it was all my fault—but it was kind of hard not to when Geri suddenly shrieked, "Fine! If that's how you feel, it's *over!*" and started storming for Chi-Chi's—I guess so she could go into the ladies' room there and have a good cry.

Scott called after her, but it was no good. Geri went tearing into the building, sobbing almost as loudly as Cara after a particularly rough mooing.

I laid down my sponge. I had a pretty good idea where *I* was going to be spending the rest of my afternoon.

But before I had a chance to go rushing off after Geri—before I had a chance to utter a single word of comfort to a visibly stricken Scott as I went by him on my way into the restaurant, before I could even so much as take a single step—Luke, who'd apparently missed the fight, went, "Man, it's hot out here."

And took off his shirt.

# Ask Annie

Ask Annie your most complex interpersonal relationship
questions. Go on, we dare you! All letters to Annie are subject
to publication in the Clayton High School *Register.* Names and
e-mail addresses of correspondents guaranteed confidential.

Dear Annie,
I am seriously in love with my best friend's
girlfriend. What do I do?
    Anonymous

Dear Anonymous,
Nothing, if you want to preserve the friendship. The only way you can make a move is
if your friend and his girlfriend break up.
Then, and only then, may you ask her out . . .
but only after a suitable period of mourning
has passed.
    Don't be surprised if your friend gets mad
at you anyway, even if you do wait until
they've broken up. Friends do not date their
friends' significant others . . . even their exes.

                           Annie

## Eight

*At first I* didn't think anything of it. You know, Luke taking his shirt off. Half the guys at the car wash had their shirts off.

So the guy took his shirt off? Big deal. I had way more important things to worry about, such as Clayton High's It Couple apparently breaking up before my very eyes and possibly—I know not solely because of, but partially, maybe—because of me.

Still, Trina's sharp intake of breath stopped me in my tracks just as I was about to race off after Geri.

I don't know why it stopped me. But it did. I stopped right where I was, then turned around slowly.

I looked at Trina. Her gaze was riveted on Luke. And not just on his truly impressive six-pack . . . the light smattering of fair hair that covered his chest before snaking down that six-pack and disappearing into the waistband of his Levi's . . .

his thoroughly impressive biceps.

Not that all of those things weren't worth staring at. Because they totally were.

No, it was the tattoo on Luke's arm, just beneath his right shoulder, that seemed to be holding Trina's attention.

The tattoo that said *Angelique.*

"Oh my Go—" Trina started to say. She didn't get to finish, however, because I slapped a hand over her mouth.

"Mmm, mmm," Trina said urgently into my palm. But I had her in a grip of iron.

"Shut up and come with me," I hissed in her ear, and started dragging her toward the doors to Chi-Chi's.

"Buh mmm," Trina tried to say, but I wouldn't let go of her.

"Girls," Mr. Hall said irritatedly as we went by, "this isn't time to play games. We have a *lot* of cars to wash."

"Yeah, I know. We'll be right out, Mr. Hall," I assured him. "We just have to go to the ladies' room."

Then I pulled Trina into the Chi-Chi's vestibule, and shoved her into the ladies' room . . .

. . . where I finally released my hand from her mouth.

"Oh my God, Jen!" she screamed. "That's Luke Striker! The new guy is *Luke Striker!*"

"Shhhh." It was taking a little while for my eyes to adjust to the darkness of the restaurant after having been out in the bright sunlight for so long. Still, I didn't need to be able to see to tell that we weren't in the rest room alone. I could hear Geri sniffling in the last stall. . . .

At least until she heard the words *Luke Striker*.

"I *knew* it!" Geri Lynn came bursting out of the stall like a bucking bronco from its pen. "I *knew* he looked familiar! Lucas is Luke Striker?"

"Listen," I said, looking from one girl to the other. Trina's face was flushed with excitement and sun. Geri's was puffy from crying. But both wore expressions of eager interest. "Okay. Yes, Lucas is Luke Striker. He's here to research a part. And Dr. Lewis himself asked me to please keep Luke's real identity a secret, so you guys have to—"

But it was like talking to a couple of two-year-olds. Because instead of a rational conversation taking place, Trina and Geri turned toward each other and started jumping up and down, shrieking at the top of their lungs: *"Luke Striker! Luke Striker! Luke Striker!"*

"Hey," I said, really afraid half the people in the restaurant were going to come running in. "Cut it out. I told you, it's supposed to be a secret—"

"Oh my God, I *knew* it was him," Trina stopped jumping long enough to say. "I knew it the other day at lunch, when he said he was a vegetarian. Because you know I stopped eating meat when I read in *Teen People* that Luke has been a vegetarian since his days on *Heaven Help Us*."

"*I* knew he was Luke Striker," Geri said, "at last night's *Register* meeting. You know, Jen, when he started talking about a celebrity's right to privacy? I swear when he said that, I was actually thinking to myself, 'You know, he looks so much like Lancelot from *Lancelot and Guenevere*, I wonder if he IS Luke Striker.'"

"You guys!" I yelled in my meanest voice, the one I only use when I'm baby-sitting and the kids start squirting ketchup at each other or whatever.

It did the trick, though. Both Trina and Geri stopped talking and looked at me.

"Listen to me," I said in a low, even voice. "Luke's real identity is supposed to be a secret. Nobody is supposed to know the truth, understand? That's how Luke wants it. He's here because he's researching a part. He can't research a part if people don't act normally around him. And if it gets out that he's really Luke Striker, nobody is going to be acting normally around him, now, are they?"

Trina and Geri exchanged glances.

"I wholly respect that," Trina said. "Luke has such deep appreciation for his craft that, as a fellow artist, I could never do anything that might in some way interfere with his creative goals. I won't say a word to anyone."

Not to be outdone, Geri made the Girl Scout sign with

her fingers. "I'll take it to the grave."

For the first time since Luke had taken his shirt off—no, since Geri had started yelling at Scott—I felt myself relax a little.

"Okay," I said. "Good. Then it's agreed. Neither of you is going to say a word to anyone about Luke not really being—"

"Oh my God," Trina said, smacking herself in the forehead. "*Why* did I tell Steve I'd go to the Spring Fling with him when I could have gone with *Luke Striker*?"

"In your dreams," Geri said. "He's taking *me*."

I couldn't believe what I was hearing. "Did you two listen to a word I just said?"

"Yeah, sure," Trina said. "Pinky swear to secrecy, yadda yadda yadda. I can still dream about him, can't I?"

"Well, I don't have a Spring Fling date anymore," Geri said, opening her purse and taking out her lipstick. "So my dreams are about to come true. I'm going to go out there and ask him right now."

I stared at Geri in horror. "Ask who? Luke? To go to the Spring Fling? But—but I thought you were going with Scott!"

"Not anymore, I'm not," Geri said, expertly applying a layer of gloss.

I couldn't believe what I was hearing. I mean, I'd suspected, but to hear her just blurt it out like that . . . "You and Scott broke up? For real? Just now?"

"That's right." Apparently satisfied by what she saw in the mirror, Geri dropped her lipstick back in her purse and turned to me. "And *don't* try to talk me into taking him back, Jen. I know you thought we were a great couple, but the truth is, it's better this way for the both of us. I'm leaving for UCLA at the end of the summer, and he's still got another year left here in Clayton, and . . . and it's just easier this way."

I could tell by the set of her jaw that Geri meant it.

Still, in spite of her warning me not to, I felt like I *had* to say something.

"But you guys have had fights before, and you've always worked it out. Maybe you should sleep on it, Geri. You might feel different after you've had some time to think about it."

"Not this time," Geri Lynn said. She reached back into her bag and pulled out her date book. *The* date book. The one she'd shown me, the one with all the hearts in it. She opened it and, taking out a pen, put a big black *X* through today's date.

I couldn't help noticing that the number of hearts on the month At-A-Glance pages had diminished somewhat drastically over the past six or seven weeks. Like, to nothing. Either Geri had slacked off recording their most intimate moments, or she and Scott hadn't had any in quite some time. . . .

Her next statement cleared up the mystery.

"No," Geri said, "this has been a long time coming, Jenny. I've felt as if Scott and I were drifting apart for some time now. We just don't have the same interests . . . the same goals. Can you believe he didn't even *want* to go the Spring Fling? He wanted to go to some anti–Spring Fling party Kwang is having—"

I knew all about Kwang's anti–Spring Fling party. I was planning on going to it myself.

"So you're just going to *ask* him?" Trina demanded. Trust Trina to completely ignore the fact that Geri's—not to mention Scott's—heart might very well be broken. All she wanted to know was what Geri's plans for Luke Striker were. "Luke, I mean? You're just going to march up to him and ask him to the Spring Fling?"

"You better believe it," Geri said, throwing back her shoulders. "Get outta the way."

"Wait a minute," Trina said. "Asking Luke Striker to the Spring Fling was *my* idea. I thought of it first!"

"But you already have a date, don't you?" Geri reminded her sweetly.

"Not for long," Trina declared, and bolted for the bathroom door.

"WAIT!" Geri practically broke her neck pelting after Trina.

I couldn't believe what I was seeing. I mean, here were two people whom I'd basically always thought of as mature young women—two people whose keen intellect and independence I had always envied and respected—and they were practically at each other's throats. Over a BOY, of all things!

"You guys," I yelled, running after them through the Chi-Chi's vestibule and then out into the parking lot. "You guys, remember, you promised not to—"

But I never got to remind Trina and Geri not to tell anyone about Luke's identity. Because by the time I caught up with them, they were standing on the outer fringes of this huge crowd that had gathered around Luke and the sedan he'd been washing.

Only now Luke was on top of the car's roof, shouting frantically into a cell phone while he tried to fend off the grasping hands of about seventy-five Troubadours, Chi-Chi's waitresses, random housewives who'd been on their way to the mall, and even a few of the guys from the pickup trucks, all of whom were screaming *"Luke! Luke! LUKE!"*

"Oh my God, you guys," I yelled at Trina and Geri as I watched Luke struggle to avoid the groping hands all around him. "What'd you *do*?"

"It wasn't us," Geri said with a shrug. "We came out and they were already at it."

"I guess I'm not the only person in Clayton who knows

about Luke Striker's Angelique tattoo," Trina said glumly.

Geri stamped her foot. "How am I going to ask him to the Spring Fling *now*? I can't get anywhere near him!"

As if that were the worst of anyone's problems! Poor Luke was about to be torn limb from limb, and all his most diehard fans could worry about was how they were going to ask him to the *Spring Fling*?

I looked up at Luke. He didn't seem scared or anything—though *I* would have been, if I were in his shoes. He'd hung up the cell phone and was trying to speak rationally to the horde of screaming women around him.

"Listen," he was saying. "You can all have autographs. Really. Just one at a time, okay?"

Nobody listened. Girls were thrusting pens and Chi-Chi's menus at him from all sides. The sopranos were the worst. Karen Sue Walters wanted Luke to sign her chest, I guess because she couldn't find any paper.

But the altos weren't behaving any better. I even saw Bored Liz—only she didn't look so bored anymore—climb up over the hood of the car and fling her arms around Luke's legs. He nearly lost his balance and fell, but Liz didn't seem to care. She was sobbing into his pant legs, crying, "Luke! Oh, Luke! I love you!"

It was way pathetic. I have to admit, I was totally embarrassed for my gender.

But the girls weren't the only ones. Even some of the guys were acting like complete fools. I heard this one guy in a John Deere baseball cap say to his friend, "I'm gonna get me an autograph and sell it on eBay!"

And Mr. Hall? Mr. Hall, a teacher who should have known better? He was the worst of all! He was screaming up at Luke, "Mr. Striker, Mr. Striker, would it be all right if I gave you the screenplay I've been working on? It's a dramedy about a young man's coming-of-age while working in the chorus of a major Broadway musical. I think you'd be perfect for the part!"

Only a couple of people in the parking lot were hanging back that I could see. One of them was Scott. He was leaning against his car, just watching, a pillar of sanity in a sea of total wackos.

I rushed over to him. I'd completely forgotten about the Geri Lynn thing. All I could think of was the fact that if somebody didn't do something, and soon, Luke was going to be torn in two, just like Mel Gibson in *Braveheart*, only by his fans, not the British.

"Do you think we should call the police?" I asked Scott worriedly. "I mean, I don't want to call the cops on my friends, but—"

But the only alternative I could see was trying to help Luke myself—except that I didn't see how I could. I mean, the crowd around the car he was standing on was about ten people deep. No way was I going to be able to get to him. . . .

"Don't worry," Scott said. "Already done."

I blinked up at him. "Already—you called the police?"

He held up his cell phone. Even as he winked at me, off in the distance I could hear the wail of a police siren.

"Oh, thank you," I said, feeling a huge wave of relief.

"So I take it he's not really enrolled," Scott said, putting his cell phone back in his pocket.

"What?" I'd been watching a Chi-Chi's waitress lunge for the autograph Luke had just given her. "Oh, no. He's just doing research for a part."

"Do Lewis and those guys know?"

"Yeah. It was their idea."

Scott shook his head. "They'll probably refuse to comment. Too bad. Still, this'll make a great story."

The fact that Scott could think about the *Register* at a time like this made me think he wasn't too concerned for Luke.

Or upset over the whole thing with Geri.

"Scott, I—"

*I'm sorry about you and Geri Lynn.* That's what I'd been going to say.

Except that right then three different things happened. The first was that a Duane County squad car pulled into the parking lot, its siren blaring. The second was that a long black limo—the same one, I guess, that picked Luke up from school every day—appeared from behind the restaurant, almost as if it had been there all along.

And the third was that Geri Lynn came running up to us, her eyes shining.

"Can you believe this?" she wanted to know. "I'm killing myself that nobody's got a camera. Something finally happens in this hick town, and we've got no way to record it!"

I couldn't tell if she'd managed to ask Luke to the Spring Fling or not. I was guessing not, as the crowd around him was still pretty thick. A lot of people had backed off at the sight of the squad car, and even more were milling away as the police officer, who was a really big guy, strolled confidently into the fray. Still, Luke hadn't gotten down from the top of the car.

"If only Kwang were here!" Geri said regretfully. "He has one of those digital cameras on his cell phone!"

The police officer had fought his way through the crowd and made it up to the car. He said something to Luke, who smiled gratefully at him, then climbed down from the car roof, while the officer held back the really diehard fans, the ones who were just not getting the point. I'm sorry to say that a good number of the sopranos, Trina among them, were in this group.

"Okay, everybody," the police officer said, as the limo pulled up in front of Luke and he swiftly dove inside it. "Show's over. Let's get this traffic moving—" Because of course every single car on Clayton Mall Road had slowed down so that its occupants could observe the strange goings-on at the Troubadour car wash.

Trina came rushing over to us. She looked flushed and upset.

"Did you see that?" she demanded. "He just got into that limo without so much as a word to anyone! I didn't even get his autograph! And after supporting him all these years—"

"Some support," I said. "You guys were practically mauling him!"

"That wasn't me," Trina said. "That was Karen Sue Walters. Did you see her, trying to get him to sign her chest? Good thing her mother isn't here—"

I noticed that, behind us, Scott and Geri had fallen into what looked to be another pretty serious conversation. I took Trina by the arm and dragged her a little bit away, so they could have some privacy. Well, relative privacy, anyway.

"Listen, if I wrote Luke a letter, could you get it to him?" Trina asked me. "I mean, the two of you must be pretty tight, if he let you in on his secret and all."

"Trina," I said, shaking my head. The limo was starting to pull away. Good thing, too, because a number of girls had rushed up to it and were plastering themselves against the tinted windows, trying to get one last look at their hero. "I barely know him. I mean, he was just here to observe—"

It was at that moment that the moonroof of the limo opened, and Luke's head and shoulders popped out. The girls around the limo screamed and leaped for him, as if they wanted to pull out fistfuls of his hair. Which, you know, is always a good way to ingratiate yourself with a guy. Not.

I thought Luke was going to throw out a few parting shots to the population of Clayton, Indiana. I thought he'd yell *See ya, suckers!* or *Thanks for nothing, pinheads!*

But that's not what he did. Instead, he looked all around the parking lot, like he'd forgotten something. Then he saw me, and yelled, "Jen!"

All heads turned in my direction.

"JEN!" Luke yelled again. And this time he accompanied the shout with an arm gesture. "COME ON!"

I felt myself turning as red as the Chi-Chi's sign.

Luke wanted me to get into the limo with him. Luke Striker wanted me to ride off into the sunset—well, not quite, since it was only like one thirty in the afternoon—with him. In his limo.

"Oh my God," I heard Trina breathe beside me. "Right. He barely knows you. That's why he's screaming your name. You, Jen. He wants *you*."

I shook my head. "No," I said. "No, it's not like that—"

Because it wasn't. His words, his accusing tone, his blazing blue eyes that day outside the ladies' room would be forever ingrained in my mind's eye. No, it wasn't like that at all.

"*JENNY!*" Luke was starting to sound frantic now.

"He wants you," Trina said again. "Why don't you go?"

But how could I go? How could I go, with all those girls crowded around his limo, shooting me the evil eye? And more police cars careening down Clayton Mall Road (the policeman had obviously called for backup)?

"For God's sake," Trina said. "*GO!*"

Then she shoved me, hard, in the back. I probably would have fallen if it hadn't been for the nice police officer, who caught me by the arm, put me back on my feet, and asked me, "Are you Jenny?"

I gave a quick nod, and the next thing I knew, the officer—still holding on to my arm—had steered me through the shrieking throng around Luke's limo, then yanked open the door to the backseat and thrust me inside. . . .

And slammed the door behind me.

Luke slithered down from the moonroof and hit the button to close it.

"Go," he yelled at the chauffeur. "Go, go, go!"

And we went.

# Ask Annie

**Ask Annie your most complex interpersonal relationship questions. Go on, we dare you! All letters to Annie are subject to publication in the Clayton High School *Register*. Names and e-mail addresses of correspondents guaranteed confidential.**

Dear Annie,
There's this boy I like. I'll call him Chuck. Anyway, Chuck says he likes me, too. But here's the thing: Chuck never calls me. I call him, like, five times a day, plus I page him at least that many times, and text message him maybe ten times a day, and e-mail him, too. But Chuck NEVER calls, pages, texts, or e-mails me. Plus his mom is starting to sound kind of mad when she picks up the phone. But how else am I supposed to keep in touch with him if he won't call me? Please help.
    I Like Chuck

Dear Like,
The reason Chuck is not calling, paging, texting, or e-mailing you is because YOU NEVER GIVE HIM THE CHANCE!!! From

your description above, it almost sounds like you're stalking the poor guy. Remember the old nursery rhyme about Little Bo-Peep? Well, nursery rhymes have some grain of truth in them. Leave Chuck alone, and he'll come home. Cool it and your guy will call. If he doesn't, well, then maybe Chuck's trying to tell you something.

Annie

## Nine

*When the nice* policeman put me in the limo with Luke Striker, I didn't know what to do—let alone what to think. I mean . . . was this a date? Did Luke Striker have a crush on me or something? I will admit that this seemed very, very unlikely, but, you know, stranger things have happened.

Except that, from everything I'd read, Luke was still smarting over Angelique Tremaine's betrayal. How could he just switch gears like that, go from liking a totally gorgeous movie star to liking . . . well, Jenny Greenley?

And couldn't he tell that I didn't like him back? At least, not that way?

Apparently not. Apparently not, because he leaned forward and said, "Let's go to the condo, okay, Pete? And lose the convoy, if you can."

I looked behind us and saw that some of the more intrepid

drivers who'd pulled up in front of Chi-Chi's to watch all the excitement were giving us the tail. I think that's what they call it. In the movies, anyway.

While this was somewhat exciting—especially when Pete started running red lights to lose them—it still didn't distract me from the problem at hand.

And that was that America's sweetheart, Luke Striker, was taking me—me, Jenny Greenley—to his condo.

"Um," I said. Because I felt like I had to say something. "You probably shouldn't have taken your shirt off."

Okay, incredibly lame, I know, but what else was I going to say?

Luke just shook his head. He wasn't even looking at me. He was looking at the countryside zipping by. We were well on our way to the lake, which was about ten miles outside of town. We'd managed to lose the entourage. Pete was a good driver. I wondered how the Duane County police were dealing with the crowd back at Chi-Chi's . . . if there'd been a riot or anything. If there had been, Scott was probably in his element. He loves anarchy of any kind.

Geri, on the other hand, was probably just mad she'd worn the wrong shoes. Or hadn't brought a camera.

"I'm getting that thing removed," Luke said bitterly.

I didn't know what he was talking about at first. Then I realized. The tattoo.

"That must've really sucked," I said from my side of the limo. I had never been inside a limo before. Can I just say—and I know it will sound stupid—but they are really big? I mean, there's this really long stretch of space between the backseat and the front seat. And in that space, at least in Luke's limo, was like a console with a bar and a TV in it. It was pretty cool. I mean, if you're the type of person who likes to watch TV in the car.

"I mean," I went on, "it must have sucked when she . . . Angelique, I mean. You know. Married that other guy."

"I don't want to talk about it," Luke said, still looking out the window. You could see the lake, now, in between the trees. Clayton Lake is man-made, but it's still really pretty. I've been boating on it, on a rented pontoon. I never actually get in the water, because I'm afraid I might run into a cadaver or something. But it's still pretty to look at.

I could understand Luke not wanting to talk about Angelique. Hey, if I'd been dating someone and all of a sudden he had just up and married someone else, I probably wouldn't want to talk about it either. So I changed the subject.

"Sorry about my friends back there," I said. "I don't know what came over them. I've never seen any of them act like that before."

Luke looked at me then, and it was like he was seeing I

was in the car with him for the first time. Then he did the strangest thing.

He smiled.

"Oh, that," he said, shaking his head. "Don't worry about it. Happens all the time. Something happens to people when they see a celebrity. It's like . . . I don't know. They don't realize we're human, just like them, or something."

I wondered if that was it. Is that why everyone had wanted to grab Luke? To make sure he was really human? Or was it just so that on Monday they could tell people in school that they'd touched Luke Striker?

"Not you, though," Luke said, startling me a little. "You're not like that. Some people are . . . different. Oh, great," he added, as the limo pulled to a stop. "We're here."

We got out in front of a modern-looking house, complete with Cape Cod shingles to make it look more New Englandy. I'd been to the condos at the lake lots of times before, because my dad designed them and my mom decorated them. Both my parents had gotten way into the nautical theme of the place. There were whitewashed rafters and shells and seagull paintings everywhere, even though there's never been a single seagull spotted at Clayton Lake. It's a big lake, but Duane County is pretty much landlocked.

"Want a soda?" Luke asked, going to the big fancy Sub-Zero fridge.

"Um," I said. The air-conditioning was on in Luke's condo. It was like twenty degrees or something. And all I was wearing was my still-damp bathing suit and a pair of shorts. I had to keep my arms crossed on account of the whole, you know, nipple thing.

For some reason all I could think of was what Luke had just said in the car. Er, the limo, I mean.

That I'm different.

"Sure, I'll have a soda," was all I said, though.

"Here ya go." Luke handed me a soda. I had to uncross one arm to get it. I'm not saying Luke noticed anything was going on up there, but he went, "Let's go out on the deck."

And to my relief, a second later he was opening the huge sliding glass doors to the deck that overlooked the lake, and we were back out in the warm sunshine.

The view from the condo was unbelievable. My dad had done a good job positioning the deck. The crystal blue lake, surrounded by thickly leafed trees, stretched out before us. There were a few sailboats out on the glassy water. The sun beat down as if it were midsummer, not spring, and birds were tweeting all over the place. It was quiet and restful and nice.

Too bad in about an hour it was going to be overrun with paparazzi. At least, it would when word got out that's where Luke Striker was staying while licking his wounds over his abandonment by Angelique Tremaine.

Luke climbed up on one of the deck railings and twisted the cap off a beer I hadn't seen him pull from the fridge. I wasn't insulted that he hadn't offered me one—I am so obviously not the type of girl anyone offers a beer to—but I was kind of wondering how he'd gotten hold of them. He isn't twenty-one, and they card like crazy in Indiana.

Then I remembered. He's a movie star. He can probably get as much beer as he wants, whenever he wants it.

"Nice out here, huh," Luke said, after he took a long pull from his beer.

I sipped my soda. It was nice and fizzy. Just the way I liked it.

"Yeah," I said.

*Different*, he'd said. *Not you. You're different.* It was driving me a little crazy, the fact that he'd asked me to come home with him. I mean, he obviously didn't want *that* from me. He could have had *that* with Trina (I'm sorry to say) or any of the other girls out there in the Chi-Chi's parking lot. Why would he have asked ME to come home with him, if sex was what he was after?

"I never went to high school," Luke said suddenly—apparently to the lake, since he certainly wasn't looking at me. "I had private tutors. We all did, all the *Heaven Help Us* kids. So except for in the movies and on TV and stuff, I never saw what a real high school was like. I thought all those John Hughes flicks were just, you know, made up. Or maybe exaggerated a little. I had no idea . . . no idea . . . that's what high school is really like."

Luke took a swig of beer, then lowered the bottle and looked at me.

"But it's not," he said. "High school—in real life—is nothing like it is in those movies. In real life, it's ten million times worse."

I just looked at him. What could I say? *Duh?* That seemed kind of rude.

"Those kids at your school," Luke said, slipping off the railing and beginning to pace the length of the deck, "are some of the rudest, most foul-mouthed, inconsiderate people I've ever met. They have— Do you know what empathy is?"

"Um," I said. "Having compassion for others?"

"Exactly. There was a consultant on *Heaven Help Us* who was a real reverend, you know, who helped with the scripts and everything? Anyway, empathy was a big thing with him. Having empathy for others. That was the first thing I noticed about Clayton High. Not a lot of people there seem capable of having empathy for the feelings of others. . . . They mercilessly torture the weak and idolize the bullies."

I did feel obligated to speak up at this point.

"That's not true," I said, since I do not, nor have I ever, idolized Kurt Schraeder. "Not everyone—"

"Oh, no, not everyone," Luke was quick to agree with me. "No, there's a large contingent of people who just sit back and watch while their friends get vilified. Those people are even worse than the bullies, in my opinion . . . and I think the reverend would agree. Because they could do something to stop it, but they're too scared to, because they don't want to be next."

I shook my head. I mean, in no way do I consider Clayton High a utopian society or anything. But we're not *that* bad.

"That is totally untrue," I said. "You saw for yourself that I went after Cara—"

"Oh, sure," Luke said. "You went *after* her. You mopped up her tears. But you didn't do anything to try to stop them from hurting her."

"What was I supposed to do?" The knot, which had disappeared from my stomach days ago, came swooping back. I couldn't believe this. He had asked me over so that he could attack my character? What *was* this? I hadn't exactly been expecting confessions of undying devotion or sweet kisses or anything, but this was just unfair. "You want me to take on the entire school? Luke, *nobody* likes Cara—"

"No," Luke said. "Nobody likes Cara. And I can't say I

blame them. I heard you in the girls' room with her. I heard what you said to her. It was good advice, probably the best she'll ever get, and she completely dismissed it. But has it ever occurred to you, Jen, that while it's true that nobody likes Cara, it's also true that everybody likes you?"

I shook my head. "That isn't—"

"Don't give me that. It's true, and you know it. Name one person who doesn't like you. Just one."

I didn't have to think very hard. I strongly suspect Mr. Hall doesn't like me. On account of my still not knowing the choreography for Luers.

And what about Kurt? Kurt Schraeder doesn't like me all that much, either. Well, he probably never thinks about me at all. But that doesn't mean when he does, it's favorably.

"Bull," Luke said, when I offered these two names up as examples.

"Okay," I said, frustrated. "Okay, let's just say everybody likes me. It's not true, but let's just say it is. So what?"

*"So what?"* Luke stopped pacing and just stared at me incredulously. *"So what?* Don't you see, Jen? You're in an incredible position. You could effect real social change at that place, and it's like you don't even realize it."

*Effect real social change?* What was he talking about?

Then it hit me. What Luke wanted. Why Luke had asked me to his place. It was so obvious, a moron could have seen it, but not me. Oh, no. Not me.

Luke was on a campaign. You know, the kind celebrities go on all the time. Like Ed Begley Jr. and his electric cars, and Pamela Anderson and PETA, and Kim Basinger and those beagles.

Luke was on a celebrity campaign to promote empathy at Clayton High School, and he wanted me in on it.

I sank down onto one of the plank benches that ran along the deck railing and went, "Oh, brother" tiredly.

"Don't *Oh, brother* me, Jen," Luke said. "You know I'm right. I've watched you, Jen. I've been doing nothing but watching you for the past four days, and the fact is, you are the only person in that whole stinking school who cares, really cares, about the people in it. Not just about yourself—in fact, I'm willing to bet that the person you think *least* of is yourself. And it's great that you care, Jen. It's really commendable. And I'm not saying that you haven't done tons to make things better. But as someone—a complete outsider—who's been watching what's going on in that school, I'm saying you could do more."

I couldn't take it. I really couldn't.

"What do you mean, *more*?" I wailed. "I do so much— I'm exhausted by the end of the day. Do you think it's so easy, being me? It isn't, you know. It's really, really hard."

"What do you mean?" Luke wanted to know, sinking

down onto the bench beside me.

"You know," I said. I couldn't believe I was telling Luke Striker—Luke Striker, of all people. Luke Striker, the hottie enigma, the one person I'd never been able to figure out. And he was now privy to my most shameful secret. It wasn't fair.

"*I'm mayonnaise,*" I whispered. Then, when he looked confused, I said in a more normal voice, "I'm what keeps the sandwich from falling apart, see? It's my job. It's what I do. I smooth things over."

"Yes," Luke said, comprehension dawning at last. He even sounded excited. "Yes, you do. That's exactly what you do!"

I didn't see what he had to be so stoked about. But I guess it's all right for him. *I'm* the one with the problem.

"But, Luke," I said, "that's *all* I am. What you're telling me . . . what you think I should do . . . I can't. I really can't."

Luke wasn't letting go, though. He was like Trina's cat, Mr. Momo, when he gets hold of a chipmunk. There is no letting go. Not until he's chewed its head off.

"But is that what you *want* to be, Jen?" Luke asked me urgently. "What do you want?"

Want? What did I *want*? Was he insane?

I decided he must be. I decided I must have been kidnapped—and was currently being held hostage—by a crazy man. It made sense, actually. Why else had I never been able to get an accurate read on him? Because he was nuts.

Wait until *People* magazine got a load of this.

"Seriously, Jen," the crazy man said. "What do you want?"

There was tons of stuff I wanted. I wanted Betty Ann back on Mrs. Mulvaney's desk where she belonged. I wanted people to quit mooing every time Cara Schlosburg walked by. I wanted out of show choir—or at least, I wanted Mr. Hall to quit yelling at me about that stupid hat and my jazz hands.

"The truth is, Jen," Luke went on, when I didn't say anything, "I don't believe you're mayonnaise at all. The way you snapped back at me that day outside the girls' room—"

I flinched, not wanting to recall that horrible moment.

But Luke wouldn't let it go.

"—I knew then there was more to you than nice little Jenny Greenley, everybody's best friend. I think you're more than mayonnaise, Jen. Much more." He'd taken the glasses off—he didn't need them anymore, since everyone knew who he really was now—and I could see that his eyes were every bit as deep, deep blue as the lake down below us.

"The truth is," he said, "I think you're special sauce."

# Ask Annie

Ask Annie your most complex interpersonal relationship questions. Go on, we dare you! All letters to Annie are subject to publication in the Clayton High School *Register*. Names and e-mail addresses of correspondents guaranteed confidential.

Dear Annie,

I just got invited to a party where I know alcohol will be served. I don't drink because I just don't like it, and I also don't like hanging around drunk people. But I don't want my friends to think I'm a wuss. What should I do?

Dry Dan

Dear Dan,

Make other plans. Then tell your friends you can't go. And stop caring so much what they think. If they don't respect your wishes, they aren't really your friends, now, are they?

Annie

*Ten*

*I know what* you're thinking. You're thinking, *So Luke Striker says you're special sauce. So what's the big deal? He's crazy, after all. And it's not like he wants to kiss you or anything.*

And it's true Luke Striker doesn't want to kiss me. Or, at least, if he does, he hasn't exactly shown any sign of it so far.

And, truthfully, if he did, would I even be very thrilled? No. Because I, unlike a lot of girls my age—who live in my own town, anyway—am not in love with Luke Striker.

I did not want Luke Striker to kiss me.

But I was starting to think he might not be so crazy after all.

Luke sent me home by myself. I guess he was worn out from all the lecturing. You know, about how I'm not living up to my potential and about how to great people comes great responsibility and about where would we be if Churchill had turned his back on his people during World War II?

It didn't cause *too* big a sensation when a big black limousine came purring down the street where I live or anything. I mean, everybody in the whole neighborhood stopped what they were doing—mowing lawns, gardening, bringing in groceries—and stared as the limo pulled up in front of my house, and I came popping out of the back. My brothers came bursting out of the house, completely freaked, wanting to know where I'd been. My mom, who'd just gotten home from a decorating gig, stood in the middle of the yard, her mouth slightly open, staring as the long black car slid away after I got out.

It was Trina who got to me first, though. She must have been watching for my return from her bedroom window, since she came tearing over from next door, her long dark hair flying behind her like a cape.

"Ohmygodohmygodohmygod," she screamed, grabbing my hands and whirling me around on my front lawn. "I cannot believe you spent a whole afternoon with *LUKE STRIKER!!!!!!*"

As soon as my brothers heard that, it was all over. I guess what had happened over at the mall hadn't quite hit the middle school set, since it seemed to be news to them. But once they'd heard the whole story—Yes, I explained. I know Luke Striker—except for some quibbling on the part of my brother Rick that I didn't get him Luke's agent's phone number—that seemed to be the extent of the interest. I mean, they're guys, after all.

My mom, after she heard the story—I left out the part about how Luke had only taken me to his condo so he could lecture me about how I wasn't living up to my potential; it had actually been a little like spending the day with a guidance counselor. If, you know, I had a guidance counselor with eyes as blue as Clayton Lake and a drop-dead gorgeous smile—went, "Well, isn't that funny," then went inside, probably to call everyone she knew to relate the tale. *You won't believe what happened to Jenny today!!*

As soon as my mom and brothers went away, Trina pulled me up onto my front porch and sat me down on the swing my dad had installed there and which my mom had decorated with cushions with—wouldn't you know it—hearts sewn on them.

"Okay," Trina said. "Now start from the beginning. What *exactly* did you and Luke talk about?"

I wasn't about to tell Trina the truth. I mean, for one thing, she just wouldn't have understood. She understands stuff like Mr. Hall's choreography—that kind of thing is no problem for her. And obviously she understands the mayonnaise thing— she's the one who called me on it in the first place.

But when it comes to stuff like—oh, I don't know, a hot movie star telling me I'm not behaving in a manner that would have made Churchill proud?—that's just not something a girl like Trina could wrap her mind around. If Luke had tried to

French kiss me? No problem. I knew I could tell Trina.

But that he'd lectured me on my responsibility as a human being to effect social change at Clayton High School? Yeah, not so much.

"Oh," I said to her, as we rocked on the swing. "You know. Just stuff. I think he's really hurting, you know. Over the Angelique thing."

I didn't know this at all—he hadn't actually mentioned the *A* word, beyond saying he was getting the tattoo removed. But it sounded good.

"He came here to get away from it all, I think," I went on. "It was totally uncool the way everybody acted, back in the parking lot."

"Tell me about it," Trina said, her eyes widening. "I couldn't believe it! Did you see the way Bored Liz grabbed his legs? Who knew she was such a slut?"

I thought it wiser not to mention the fact that Trina had only acted maybe one iota better.

"Did he mention me at all?" Trina wanted to know.

"Um. Not really."

"What about Geri? Did he mention Geri? Because she slipped him her number, and she so thinks he's going to call."

"Um," I said uncomfortably. "No. Are she and Scott still broken up? Because when I left, they seemed to be . . . talking."

"Oh, please," Trina said. "The two of them are so over.

I'm surprised they lasted as long as they did. Geri's so bossy! I think Scott just stuck it out with her to keep from hurting her feelings, you know? I mean, seeing as how she's going off to college in a few months anyway. He's nice, that way."

Yes, he is.

"So I am totally breaking up with Steve after the movie tonight," Trina went on. "I thought about calling it off before the movie, but I really want to see this one, and I'm totally broke. Do you think that's really heartless? But, I mean, is it my fault he always insists on paying?"

Um, yes. I felt bad for poor Steve, whose only crime was loving a girl who didn't love him back.

But I didn't say anything, because it would have just made Trina mad.

Then I remembered what Luke and I had talked about. About how I was always smoothing things over, instead of keeping them from happening in the first place. Wasn't my not saying anything about Trina using Steve for free movie tickets exactly what Luke had been talking about? This was an injustice . . . a total mistreatment of Steve.

And I was just sitting there letting it happen. Because I'm nice little Jenny Greenley, everybody's best friend.

I knew how it would go, of course. Trina would dump Steve, and then I'd spend the entire bus ride up to Luers comforting him.

Well, not this time. I don't know—maybe that whole thing Luke had said to me, about me being special and all, had gone to my head.

Or maybe I'd just decided to grow a backbone for a change.

Whatever the reason, I decided to give it a try. Luke's theory of me effecting social change. Right then and there. If it turned out Luke was wrong, well, no big loss. But if he was right . . .

If he was right, things were going to start changing around here.

And about time, too.

"Why are you going to break up with Steve?" I asked Trina.

She blinked at me. "Duh," she said. "So I can go to the Spring Fling with Luke, silly."

"What makes you think Luke would go to the Spring Fling with you?" I demanded.

Trina looked worried. "Why? Do you think Geri's already asked him? Did he say yes?"

"What makes you think," I asked, getting up from the swing and beginning to pace the length of the porch, the same way Luke had paced his deck, "that Luke would go to the Spring Fling with anyone from this town, after what we did to him today? How do you know he's not heading straight back to L.A.?"

Trina knit her brow. "Jen? Are you all right?"

"You know what? No, I'm not." Because I'm sick of being nice little Jenny Greenley, everybody's best friend. I want to be nice to people. Yes, it's true.

But I also want people to be nice back. Not just to me, but to *each other*, for a change.

"I'm not all right," I said to Trina. "The way you treat Steve, Trina. It's wrong."

"Steve?" Trina laughed. "I thought we were talking about Luke. What's wrong with you, Jen?"

"I'll tell you what's wrong with me," I said, feeling just like I had outside the ladies' room with Luke—sick to my stomach but plunging on anyway. Because I had to. I just had to. "I've stood by and watched you treat Steve like dirt for too long. He has feelings, you know. He's a human being, and he happens to be in love with you, and it's uncon-scionable of you to take advantage of that for free movie tickets and supersize tubs of popcorn."

"Unconscionable?" Trina echoed. "What does that mean? What is *with* you? We're talking about *Steve*, remember?"

"He has feelings, too, you know. If you don't love him— and I don't believe you do, because if you did, you wouldn't be breaking up with him a week before Spring Fling so you can ask someone else—then tell him that. It's not fair to get his hopes up. You're just using him, and it's not right."

Trina laughed. I'm serious. My first stab at effecting social change, and I got laughed at. It hadn't been easy, either. My heart was beating really fast, my palms were unpleasantly sweaty, and my stomach really, really hurt.

But I'd *had* to say it. Really, after everything Luke had said, what choice did I have?

"Who died," Trina wanted to know, "and made you Steve McKnight's baby-sitter? He's a big boy, Jen. I think he can take care of himself."

"Not where you're concerned," I shot back. "Because where you're concerned, he has a weak spot, and you're taking advantage of it. And it's going to stop after today, because either you decide he's the one, or you tell him the truth. Because if you don't, I . . . I'll tell him myself!"

"What is wrong with you?" Trina demanded, standing up. The swing jiggled around behind her. "What, are you jealous or something? God, my mother warned me this was going to happen someday. My mom said someday you were going to get jealous over the fact that I always have a date and you don't. She was like, 'Don't rub it in Jenny's face, Catrina.' But I was like, 'Jen's not like that, Mom. She's happy for me. She doesn't care that I have a boyfriend and she doesn't.' But I guess it turns out my mother was right, huh, Jen? Because that's what this is about, isn't it? The fact that I've got a date for the Spring Fling, and you don't."

"Oh, I've got a date for the Spring Fling," I assured her.

"Oh, right," Trina said with a laugh. And not a very nice one, either. "With who?"

"With Luke Striker."

Trina flinched as if I'd punched her. *"WHAT?"*

And the scary thing was, it was true. I wasn't even lying. I *did* have a date to the Spring Fling. And it was with Luke Striker.

Nobody could have been more stunned than me by the way it had come about, either. It had happened in the weirdest way. The two of us had been sitting there on his deck, exhausted, I think, by our long talk. Luke had gone inside and gotten himself another beer and me a soda. We'd been sitting there for some minutes in fairly companionable silence when the phone inside the condo started to ring. A second later, there was a knock at the condo door.

"Well," Luke said, taking a swig from his beer. "Guess the jig is up."

"Wow," I said, a little shocked at how fast they'd managed to find him. "That's kind of scary."

"Not really," Luke said. "I mean, I'm used to it. It's you I feel bad for."

*"Me?* What are you worried about *me* for?"

"'Cause they're gonna come after you, too," he said,

"when the full story gets out. You're gonna have Nancy O'Dell and Pat O'Brien beating a path to your door, too."

"Aw," I said. "I'll be all right."

He looked at me then, long and hard. Then he said, "You know what? I think you will. Listen. I feel bad, inviting you over, then doing nothing but yell at you."

"That's all right," I said. "I think I see what you were getting at. And it's something I'll try to work on. I'm not making any promises, but . . . I'll try."

"Glad to hear it." Inside the house, the phone rang and rang. The knocking grew louder. "But it's still not all right. Let me make it up to you. I know. Let me take you to the Spring Fling."

I just about spat my soda out all over him. I managed to swallow it instead, but of course it went down the wrong tube. The next thing I knew, soda was coming out of my nose, and tears were streaming down my face because the soda stung so badly. I was beginning to see why Geri Lynn liked her soda flat. That way, if it went up her nose, it probably didn't hurt as much.

"Hey, you okay?" Luke was patting me on the back, thinking I was choking. "Here, here's a napkin."

I sopped up soda and tears with the napkin, then laughed.

"Oh my God," I said. "Sorry about that. I thought you said

. . . you know, I thought you just asked me to the Spring Fling."

"I did," Luke said.

My heart gave a lurch. Not a good lurch, either, but like an *Uh-oh, I think I'm about to get hit by that bus* kind of lurch.

Because, really, the last thing I needed was to go to the Spring Fling with a teen heartthrob. I have enough problems without having to fight off a bunch of girls just to share a glass of punch with my own date.

"Before you say no, hear me out," Luke said, as if he'd been reading my mind. "For one thing, it won't be like today. That was really bad back there, I admit. But it's because people weren't expecting it. If we go to the Spring Fling together, it'll be different. Yeah, there might be some photographers or something, but everybody'll know I'm with you, so they won't . . . you know. Be throwing themselves at me. At least, not as much."

All I could do was stare at him. I really thought maybe the beer had gone to his head or something. Or maybe there was a camera hidden somewhere, and this was one of those reality shows. And in a second Ashton Kutcher or somebody was going to pop out and tell me I'd been punked. . . .

"The thing is," Luke went on, "like I told you, I never went to high school. So I never got to go to a school dance. And I want to see what it's like. I'll admit there's a prom scene in the next project I'll be working on, but that's not why I want to go. I want to go for me, really. So I won't have missed out on anything."

"Missed out on anything?" I shook my head. "Luke, you've been to, like, Africa. You've been to Europe, what, a thousand times? You sat next to Clint Eastwood at last year's Oscar ceremony. I saw you there—don't deny it. How could you have *missed out* on anything?"

"Easy," Luke said. "I miss out on everything normal people get to do. Jen, I can't even go to the grocery store to buy milk without people wanting my autograph. Is it so wrong that I want to experience something every American teen but me has?"

Every American teen has NOT experienced the Spring Fling. I mean, look at me, for instance.

But I didn't want to burst his bubble. At least, not that way. What I really wanted to do was get real about what was bothering me the most. . . .

"But why ME?" I asked him. "I mean, you could go to the Spring Fling with anybody. Trina is much prettier than me, and she wants to go with you. . . ."

"Yeah," Luke said. "But Trina's not my friend, is she?"

I stirred on the bench uncomfortably. "Well. No."

"And Trina doesn't like me as just a friend—the way you do—does she?"

I understood then. I knew why Luke was asking me. I

knew *what* he was asking me, too.

And my heart swelled with pity for him. I know, it's ridiculous—*me*, feeling sorry for a millionaire, a movie star who was worshiped by women all over the world, and who had his own Ferrari.

But there was one thing money and good looks couldn't buy Luke Striker. And that was friendship. Genuine friendship, from someone who didn't want to use him to get rich or famous herself, from someone who liked him for who he was, not the characters he played on the screen. All he wanted was to be treated like a normal person.

And really, if you think about it, what's more normal than the Spring Fling?

He had urged me not to be little Jenny Greenley, everybody's friend anymore. He had told me I had the potential to be something special.

But it looked like I was going to have to perform one last act of Jen Greenley niceness.

And I was going to have to do it for him. Even if he didn't realize that's why I was doing it.

"Sure," I said gently. "Sure, I'll go to the Spring Fling with you, Luke."

He had looked excited—genuinely excited—at the idea. Of going to the Spring Fling. With *me*.

The poor guy.

"Cool!" he said, leaping up from the bench. "Look, I'll probably fly back to L.A. after this. . . ." He meant the ringing phone and steady pounding on the door. "But I'll come back next weekend to take you. To the Spring Fling, I mean. Well, really, you'll be taking me, since it's your school and all, but—"

"I'll look forward to it," I said, smiling at his enthusiasm. It reminded me of the time Jake, his character on *Heaven Help Us*, learned a valuable lesson about helping the homeless, spending his Christmas at a soup kitchen, then came home to find a mountain bike some rich member of his dad's church had bought for him as a reward.

Because, you know, if you help the homeless, of course someone will buy you a mountain bike. Not.

And then the reporters—because that's who'd been knocking at the door, it turns out. Someone had evidently heard about the near-riot at the mall on their police scanner and called the tabloids—came stumbling around the back of the condo, calling Luke's name and snapping our photo as we stood out there on the deck.

That's when we ducked, laughing, back into the house, and when Luke finally sent me home, with the assurance he'd be back next Saturday night to pick me up at seven.

An assurance that Trina, standing on my front porch an hour later, clearly didn't believe.

"No way," she said. "No way. There is *no way* you are

going to the Spring Fling with Luke Striker. *No way.*"

"Fine," I said. "Don't believe me. But about Steve, Trina. What's it gonna be? Because I'm really tired of cleaning up after you every time you dump him."

Trina's face, which was totally normal one second—well, transfixed with rage, but otherwise normal—collapsed the next. Seriously. She just burst into tears.

"How c-could you?" she wailed. "How could you agree to go to the Spring Fling with him, when you know—you know how I feel about him?"

"Trina," I said. "You barely know him. You're not in love with *him* at all. You're in love with Lancelot. Or Tarzan. Or worse, the kid he played on *Heaven Help Us.*"

Trina threw both her hands up over her face and, sobbing as loudly as Cara Schlosburg ever had, ran from my porch over to hers. When she got there, she yanked open her front door and ran inside, screaming, "Mom!" in a semi-hysterical manner.

A second later, my own mother came out onto our own porch and said worriedly, "What was all that screaming? Was that Trina?"

"Yes," I said miserably.

"What on earth did you say to her?" my mom wanted to know.

"The truth."

# Ask Annie

**Ask Annie your most complex interpersonal relationship questions. Go on, we dare you! All letters to Annie are subject to publication in the Clayton High School *Register*. Names and e-mail addresses of correspondents guaranteed confidential.**

Dear Annie,

There's a girl in school who is always competing with me. Like whenever we get our tests back, she always wants to know what I got on mine, and if she got a better grade, she acts like it's this big deal. She always wants to know what topics I've chosen for my research papers, and when I tell her, she picks the same topics! Then she always wants to see who did better. It's really annoying. How can I make her stop?

Doing Her Own Work

Dear Work,

Easy. Stop telling her what grades you got. And quit telling her your research topics as well. She can't play the game if she doesn't have anybody to play with, now, can she?

Annie

## Eleven

*That dude with* the white hair, the one who painted the Campbell's soup cans? Yeah, that one. He said everybody gets fifteen minutes of fame.

Well, he was wrong. Because I got a lot more than a mere fifteen minutes that week after the car wash.

The E! network devoted more than fifteen minutes to the story that first day alone. And you should have seen the various tabloid headlines:

Small Time Town Gets Visit from Big-Time Star
Hunk Undercover!
Luke Goes Local
High School Heartthrob
Stud in Study Hall!

It went on and on. Suddenly, Clayton, Indiana—which you can't even find on most maps—was in the limelight.

Journalists descended upon our little town like those winged monkeys in *The Wizard of Oz*. You couldn't turn a corner, it seemed like, without running into Lynda Lopez or Claudia Cohen.

And I'm not going to deny that it wasn't a little cool, at first. Everybody, it seemed like, wanted an exclusive interview with me, the girl who'd shown Luke Striker what it was like to be a real teen.

And when word that Luke and I were going to the Spring Fling together got out, which it did, and plenty fast—I saw Trina on the Style network, telling some reporter, "Yeah, Jen's my best friend. She's going to the Spring Fling with him"—the requests for interviews came rolling in so fast, my dad finally took the phone off the hook.

Because, you know, it wasn't like I could *do* any of these interviews. I mean, Luke's my friend.

You don't go on TV and talk about your friend.

Oh, sure, when somebody shoved a microphone in front of me as I was getting off the bus to school in the morning or whatever, and went, "Jenny Greenley, was it hard keeping Luke Striker's true identity a secret?" I'd answer them, just to be polite. I'd be like, "No."

Or "Jenny Greenley, can you tell us what you're wearing to the dance?" I was all, "Oh, you know, a dress." (A dress my mom picked up for me at L.S. Ayres, because I couldn't go to the mall for fear of being mobbed by worshipful tweens. Because it turns out if you're going to the Spring Fling with Luke Striker, that kind of makes you a celebrity, too.)

And when I got cornered by this reporter from *Teen People*, who asked me, "What's the truth about your relationship with Luke Striker? Are you two in love?" I was all, "You know what? We're just really good friends."

Because that was the truth.

But whatever. I wasn't going to sit down for an in-depth chat about Luke with *Regis and Kelly* (even though, you know, they asked me to, but what—I was going to fly to New York?).

The funniest part about the whole thing was the people at school. They didn't feel the same compunction I did about not talking about Luke to reporters. You should have seen Karen Sue Walters on Fox TV, going on about how Luke had given her tips on her solo in "Day by Day." Yeah, whatever, Karen Sue. I happened to know Luke had said maybe two words to her, and those words had been, "Nice song."

But she was making out like he was her vocal coach or whatever and that this was her ticket to stardom.

Even Mr. Hall got in on the act. He snapped up every interview that came his way and always ended each one with, "And the Troubadours will be performing at the Bishop Luers Show Choir Invitational—that's Bishop Luers—this Friday. Try to stop by!"

Yeah, whatever, Mr. H. I'm sure all of America wants to see the Troubadours warbling out "As Long as He Needs Me" (I'll Klingon Steadfastly).

Still, it got old pretty fast, the reporter thing. By like the third day, I was over it. I was over Trina's being mad at me, too. She was all, "Oh, Jen's my best friend," to the cameras but totally giving me the cold shoulder in person. It seemed like she couldn't forgive me for

a) calling her on the Steve thing, and
b) agreeing to go to the Spring Fling with Luke.

There was one other thing she couldn't forgive me for, even though it wasn't my fault. In fact, I had nothing whatsoever to do with it. And that's that Steve—good old dependable Steve—had gotten tired of listening to Trina whine about Luke Striker . . .

. . . and dumped her.

Yeah. Dumped Trina. And told me at lunch—he started eating with us, while Trina stayed in the choir room—that he didn't regret it a bit. He was going to Kwang's Anti–Spring Fling party, and couldn't have been happier to have his freedom at last.

Geri Lynn, though, didn't seem as happy about her decision to give her own soul mate the heave-ho. It wasn't that she was unhappy about having broken up with Scott. It was more like she was unhappy that Scott wasn't more upset about it. Every time I saw her, she started asking me searching questions about Scott. Did I think he liked someone else already? Because she had the feeling he liked someone else, and that's why he hadn't protested at all when she'd dropped the hammer on him. Didn't that mean he must like someone else? Had he said anything to me about it? Not that she cared, but . . .

The truth was, back before that day at Luke's place, I might have coddled Geri along. I might have been all, *Why, no, Geri Lynn, he hasn't said anything to me. But I'm sure he's still hurting from the breakup. If you miss him so much, why don't you call him and ask him to come over? You two were so great together, you should really get back together.*

No way. Now I just went, "You know what, Geri? You broke up with him. It's over. Move on."

Geri's eyes got all big, and she looked like she was going to cry, so I had to apologize afterward (even though I still didn't say I thought they should get back together).

But she didn't try to talk to me about it anymore. Which was such a relief.

But it was the thing with Cara that really got everybody talking about me. I mean, at first it was just Trina. You know, complaining to anyone who would listen that ever since I'd gotten asked to the Spring Fling by Luke Striker, I'd "changed."

Then, after what I said to Geri about moving on, *she* started in on it, too. *What's wrong with Jen? Is Jen okay? She's acting so* strangely. . . .

Nobody came right out and said it in front of me, but I knew it was happening. Voices fell silent whenever I walked into the ladies' room, a sure sign I'd been the topic of conversation.

And at the lunch table, people steered far from the subject weighing most heavily on everyone's minds: Luke Striker.

The only person at school who treated me at all normally anymore—well, besides Mr. Hall, who still yelled at me about my jazz hands—was Scott. Scott went on being the same old Scott, taking over whenever he didn't like what I was doing with the layout of the paper, helping me pick out which Ask Annie letters to print, making fun of whatever book I'd most recently loaned him, offering me bites of his homemade tortellini with four-cheese sauce at lunchtime. . . .

Scott was still just . . . Scott.

Even my parents were treating me differently. I don't know if it was on account of knowing I'd been invited to a school dance—the first time this had ever happened—or if it was *who* had invited me. In any case, suddenly they started treating me as if I were closer to their age than to Cal's or Rick's. For instance, my dad asked me when I wanted to go down to the Department of Motor Vehicles to get my learner's permit, something he'd never once brought up before, for fear, I'd always been sure, that he might actually have to get into a car with me behind the wheel.

My mom, meanwhile, surprised me by saying one morning over her corn flakes, as if I were a friend of hers and not her daughter, "I wish you'd ask Cara Schlosburg to go to the movies or something with you, Jenny. Her mother was telling me at the Y yesterday that Cara's been very down lately. She even asked her parents if they'd look into getting her a transfer to the girls' military academy over in Culver next fall."

Military academy! *Cara?* I was shocked. I mean, I didn't blame Cara for wanting to go to school someplace where people wouldn't moo at her.

But *military* school? Clayton High is bad, but not as bad as *military* school.

Or was it?

All I knew for sure was that, if it was, it wasn't going to be that way for long.

I knew I didn't have any time to lose, so I didn't procrastinate. I walked up to Cara at lunch the very day my mom mentioned the Culver thing and asked, "What are you doing after school today?"

Cara had been nibbling on a lettuce leaf, pretending that was all she was going to eat for lunch. I knew, of course, that she had a locker full of Little Debbie snack cakes and that she'd be chowing down on them as soon as she thought no one was looking. I'd walked by and seen her doing it.

She looked up at me and went, *"Me?"* Then she glanced behind her, as if to make sure I was really speaking to her and not someone else. "Um. Nothing. Why?"

"Because I need to talk to you about something," I said. "Can I come over to your house?"

She looked as shocked as I'd felt when my mom had dropped the bomb about Culver. A wave of guilt washed over me when I realized that I was probably the first person—ever—to ask Cara if I could come over to her house.

*"You* want to come over to my house?" Now Cara looked suspicious, as if she thought I might be playing a trick on her. "What for?"

"I told you," I said. "I need to talk to you about something. What bus do you take?"

"Number thirty-five," Cara said. "It leaves from school at three ten. But—"

"See you at three ten," I said. And I turned around to go back to my table.

"Wait a minute." Cara's face was slowly turning red. I guess because she was starting to realize how many people had been observing our conversation. I am, after all, going to the Spring Fling with Luke Striker. You could say that I attract a certain amount of attention from my peers everywhere I go. "Are you sure . . . are you sure this isn't some kind of mistake?"

"I'm sure," I said. And walked away.

I had to skip my after-school *Register* meeting in order to fit Cara into my schedule, but I figured the paper could get along without me for one day. Cara, I knew, needed me more.

As soon as I got to her house, I saw that my job was going to be easier than I'd imagined. That's because it turned out Cara lived in a totally normal house—not a trailer, with moonshine-mixing parents, as was rumored—but a blue-gray split-level with white gingerbread trim and potted geraniums along the driveway.

Mrs. Schlosburg, who greeted us at the door with a plate of still warm-from-the-oven chocolate chip cookies (Cara had obviously called ahead to warn her mother that she was bringing home a guest), was an attractive woman in a Talbots sweater—no missing teeth, no pack-a-day habit, as had been rumored—who went out of her way to make me feel welcome. I should've figured as much, seeing how she belongs to the same aquasize class set my mother does. She kept asking me if there was anything I wanted—anything at all—and letting me know I was totally welcome to stay for dinner.

I could perfectly understand Mrs. Schlosburg's enthusiasm. Being the girl-next-door type, I am very much a favorite among the parental set. It's sickening but true.

But Mrs. Schlosburg had no idea that it wasn't the girl next door she was dealing with. Oh, no.

The first thing I did when Cara showed me to her room—which was every bit as frilly as my own—was fling open her closet door and pull out all the capri pants that I found hanging there.

"What are you doing?" Cara asked curiously.

"I once told you to be yourself," I said. "And you told me you don't know who that is. Well, I'm going to show you. Go wash your hair."

Cara just stared at me. "But—"

"Go get in the shower."

"But—"

"Do it."

Somewhat to my surprise, Cara did as I told her. I had to hand it to Luke. For a guy I couldn't figure out to save my life, he'd sure figured out *me*. I was a natural born leader. It was like in my blood or something.

I was still going through her closet, nibbling on the chocolate chip cookies Mrs. Schlosburg had brought me, when Cara emerged from the bathroom in a towel, her hair curling damply around her face.

She looked from me to the mounting pile of clothes on her bed.

"What are you doing?" she wanted to know.

"These you may wear to school," I said, indicating the things I'd left hanging in her closet. Most of them were what my mom would call fashion *classics*—some button-down shirts, a jeans skirt, a few sweaters, a couple of pairs of flat-front khakis—darker shades only—black jeans, a pair of Nike's, some clogs, a cute pair of platform sandals, and a few A-line skirts.

"These," I said, gesturing to the three-foot pile of capri pants, miniskirts, halter tops, cargo pants, and low-riders—clothes my mom would have labeled as *trendy*—"you should really give to Goodwill. I know Courtney and those guys wear clothes like these. But just because something is in style doesn't mean it's right for you. It's more important to look good than to look fashionable."

Cara stared at me. "But isn't that the same thing?"

I could see we had a long road ahead of us.

After that, it was time to work on Cara's hair. I had spent enough time around Trina—who dyes her own locks every chance she gets—to know what a difference mousse and a few well-placed highlights could do. I decided—since Cara said she didn't know—that she should go auburn. Not red. Nothing too flashy. Just a deep, interesting, Mary-Jane-from-Spider-Man auburn.

I hadn't come armed only with beauty products, of course. I knew I couldn't just give Cara a makeover and call it a day. I had also brought over some of my favorite books and DVDs, including the later seasons of *Buffy the Vampire Slayer*. One of Cara's problems had always seemed to me to be that she wasn't the world's best conversationalist. You can't blame her, really, since the only people she ever hung around—not that they ever actually spoke to her, but whatever—were girls like Courtney Deckard, who talk more about *things*—après sun cream, the Zone—than *ideas*. Boring.

I thought it might help if, while I was improving Cara's looks, I tried to improve her mind. Just a little. So she'd have something to talk with people about. Besides her diet, that is.

Plenty of mousse, a spritz of hair spray for volume, a general toning down of the whole eyeliner thing, and a lot of covering up what she used to let all hang out later, and Cara was transformed. She'd gone from *why me?* to *look at me!* in just a couple of hours. By the time I finally got through with her, Mr. Schlosburg had gotten home from work. So I had him and Mrs. Schlosburg sit in the living room, then "presented" the new and—in my opinion, anyway—improved Cara to them.

The completely stunned expressions on their faces were all the proof I needed that I had done a good job. Mrs. Schlosburg even took photos.

I accepted the Schlosburgs' invitation to take me to dinner at Clayton Inn, Clayton, Indiana's fanciest restaurant (the place where the Spring Fling would be held). I figured it would be a good opportunity to give Cara her next lesson . . . that it was healthier to fill up on a rib eye and baked potato at dinner than it was to nibble a dinky salad with no dressing, only to scarf down seven hundred Little Debbie snack cakes later in the evening. From now on, I instructed Cara, she was to eat three full—but healthy—meals a day. No more plates of iceberg in the caf, please.

Where, I informed her, she'd be sitting at my table from now on . . . a statement which caused her eyes to go very wide.

By the time Mr. and Mrs. Schlosburg dropped me off at home, they were both gushing with appreciation over my having taken their daughter under my wing. I have to admit that made me a little uncomfortable. Oh, not that they were so deeply touched or anything. But the fact was, I ought to have stepped in and taken Cara under my wing long before I finally had. I'd let her flounder around by herself for far, far too long.

But, I told myself, as I got ready for bed, all that was changing. Cara wasn't the only one undergoing a transformation.

Buh-bye, nice little Jenny Greenley, everybody's best friend. Hello, Jen, effector of social change.

And anybody who hadn't realized it by noon the next day certainly knew it by the end of lunch. That's when Cara and I made our entrance to the caf.

She had, I was satisfied to see, forgone the blow-drying that morning. Her newly darkened hair sprung in naturally curly waves all around her face, framing it beautifully. What little makeup she had on enhanced instead of smothered. And there appeared to be a new spring in her step that I couldn't remember ever having seen before.

Standing outside the cafeteria doors, where we'd agreed to meet, Cara tugged on her split-sleeved blouse and made sure the hem of her knee-length—no more minis: some things a girl should keep a mystery—rayon skirt was even. I reached up and adjusted an auburn curl so that it lay insouciantly across one shoulder.

"Ready?" I asked her.

Cara nodded nervously. Then she said, "Can I ask you something first though, Jen?"

"Shoot," I said.

Cara's gaze was steady. "Why . . . why are you doing this for me?"

I had to think about that one for a second. I couldn't say anything about Culver, because I didn't want her to know that her mother had been talking to mine about her. And of course I couldn't say anything about how Luke had told me that it was the job of people like me to help people like her.

Except that, when I really thought about it, I realized that neither of those were the reason why I'd helped Cara. I'd helped Cara because . . .

"Because I like you, Cara."

Maybe I'd realized it a little late. But it was still true.

So that's what I said, with a shrug.

Except maybe I should have kept that information to myself, because Cara's eyes filled up with tears, jeopardizing her mascara. . . .

"Oh my God!" I cried. "Stop it!"

"I can't help it," Cara said, starting to sniffle. "That's the nicest thing anyone's ever said to me—"

I couldn't get those cafeteria doors open fast enough.

"In!" I commanded, pointing imperiously.

The din hit us with as much force as the scent of today's special—turkey chili. I felt Cara take a step backward, jolted by the roar.

But retreat was not an option. I reached behind me, found a clammy hand, and pulled.

We were inside. And heading down the catwalk.

*Don't hesitate*, I'd advised Cara the night before. *If you hesitate—if you show so much as an instant of indecision—they'll attack. Remember, I'll be right there with you. Keep your gaze straight ahead. Don't slouch. Don't shuffle.*

*And for the love of God, don't make eye contact.*

I was trying to play it casual, so I didn't look at Cara. I had no idea whether or not she was following my instructions.

But I could tell by the slowly decreasing decibel level in the room that something was happening. People were pausing mid-conversation. Soon, you couldn't even hear a fork scrape. Silence—for the first time in the history of Clayton High School—reigned in the cafeteria. The only sound I could hear were those of my own footfalls . . . and the click-clack of Cara's platform sandals.

I risked a glance at Cara then. Her cheeks were turning as pink as her blouse.

But to my relief, she didn't waver.

She didn't hesitate.

And she didn't make eye contact.

I stooped and picked up two trays. I handed one to her. We made our way down the concession line. I took a bowl of turkey chili, a tossed salad—with the dressing on it—some cornbread, a diet soda, and an apple. Cara did the same. The lunch ladies eyed us, but not because of our food choices.

They eyed us because they, like me, had never heard the place so quiet.

Only they, unlike me, could not figure out why no one was speaking.

We moved toward the cashier. We paid. We picked up our trays. And we started for our seats.

If anything was going to happen, I knew, it was going to happen then, right at that moment. Cara's transformation from wannabe to I'm Just Me was remarkable, but a dye job and makeup—even a full-length top—would not make a lick of difference to a bully determined to keep Cara under his— or her—heel. They'd had time to recover from the shock now. The taunts—if there were to be any—would come now.

Four feet. Ten feet. Twenty. *Made it.* We had successfully placed our trays on the table and were pulling back our chairs when it happened.

A moo.

Cara froze. The moo had come from behind us. I had drilled into her the night before the instruction that if any-one mooed at her, ever again, she was not to react. She was not to burst into tears. She was not to run from the room. She was to go on as if she hadn't heard it. She was not to so much as turn her head.

But would she? Had all my coaching fallen on deaf ears? I watched apprehensively as Cara's fingers tightened on her chair back . . . tightened until her knuckles went white.

Then she pulled the chair out, sat down in it, and began calmly to eat her chili.

Relief coursed through my body like ice water on a hot day. I almost felt giddy. Yes! The spell was broken! Cara would never be mooed at again.

Until I heard it again. *Mooooo.*

Scott Bennett, the only one at our table who'd gone on eating as if nothing was happening the whole time Cara and I had been approaching the table, paused with a forkful of what looked to me like chicken enchilada halfway to his lips. He glanced in the direction of the moo, which seemed to have come from Kurt Schraeder's table. I, too, looked in that direction. I saw Kurt looking right back at me, a devious little smile on his face.

"Do you," I inquired acidly, my voice—because it was the only one in the caf—carrying easily the thirty feet to Kurt's table, "have a problem, Kurt?"

"Yeah," Kurt started to say.

But then he broke off when Courtney Deckard elbowed him hard in the ribs.

I looked at Courtney. Courtney looked at me.

I'll tell you the truth. I don't know if it was the fact that at the end of the week, I was going to be going to the Clayton High School Spring Fling with Luke Striker, and

Courtney knew it, or if Luke's special sauce theory really had some merit.

All I know is, right after that, Courtney picked up her diet soda and said something to the girl next to her. The girl next to her responded. Then everyone at their table started eating and chatting again, as if nothing had happened. Soon the entire population of the cafeteria was doing the same.

Including, I was pleased to see as I sat down, Cara Schlosburg, who was politely asking Kwang if he had happened to watch *Buffy*, and if so, did he, or did he not, think that show jumped the shark after Angel had left it.

My heart swelled. There was not another single moo.

Cara Cow, I saw, was dead. Long live Cara Schlosburg.

Yes, I thought to myself, as I dug into my chili, suddenly starving. *Yes!*

# Ask Annie

Ask Annie your most complex interpersonal relationship questions. Go on, we dare you! All letters to Annie are subject to publication in the Clayton High School *Register*. Names and e-mail addresses of correspondents guaranteed confidential.

Dear Annie,

The only thing my dad is interested in is sports. He never paid any attention to me when I was taking ballet and art and stuff, but now that I'm on a sports team, it's like he couldn't be prouder of me.

But here's the thing: I totally hate sports. I only tried out for the team to make him happy. I never thought I'd actually get on it. I stuck with it because I figured maybe I'd learn to like it. Didn't happen. I hate the practices and I hate the games. I want to quit. The only problem is, my dad says once you've accepted a position on a team, you can't quit, because you'll be letting the team down. I'm thinking, screw the team. I want to get back to ballet. What's your advice, Annie?

Soccer Sucks

Dear Sucks,

Life's short. The fact that you hate the sport so much means there's no way you'll be playing up to your potential. The team would actually be better off if you quit and they found someone willing to play with heart. Tell your dad that you know he's trying to teach you good values, but that if you don't try new things, you'll never know what you're best at. And you can only make time for new things by quitting the things you KNOW don't work for you.

Then prepare yourself for the I'm-very-disappointed-in-you" speech. But don't worry. He'll get over it. When he sees you doing grand jetés at your first big ballet recital.

Annie

# Twelve

*Okay, I'll admit* it. After the Cara thing, I kind of started to think maybe Luke had been right about me.

Because it worked. It totally worked.

And, yeah, maybe it worked because you could still see clips of me on *Access Hollywood* every night, going, "No, really, Luke and I are just friends."

But whatever. It had worked. People stopped mooing at Cara.

And, sure, a lot of people went around going—including, I heard through the grapevine, my ex–best friend Trina— "What's with Jen? Why is she being so nice to Cara Cow?"

But never within earshot of Cara, so I didn't care.

Especially when my mother reported to me that after school that first day—the day she walked down the catwalk without being mooed at—Cara informed Mrs. Schlosburg that she'd signed up to join next year's student council.

So it didn't look as if she'd be heading off to Culver anytime soon.

It was just too bad that while I'd managed to influence Cara's life so positively, I was still my best friend's least favorite person. Trina continued to refuse to talk to me, and, I'll admit, it was taking its toll. I missed her. Without Trina to chat with online, doing my Latin homework wasn't half as much fun. I didn't regret saying what I'd said to her, and I still didn't think my agreeing to go to the Spring Fling with Luke Striker was the huge betrayal she evidently thought it was.

But I wish I had handled the situation a little better. Because being on the outs with Trina was affecting my life in a pretty negative way . . . especially during Troubadour rehearsals.

The day of the big show choir invitational was fast approaching. Our dresses—the hundred and eighty dollar ones—arrived, in all their red, sequined glory. They were truly the most hideous garments I had ever seen—the kind of dress that, if I'd found something similar in Cara's closet, would have gone straight in the Goodwill pile. . . .

And probably even Goodwill wouldn't have wanted it.

But Mr. Hall loved them. When we stood on the risers for our first dress rehearsal, during class on Tuesday, he actually got teary eyed. He said that, at last, we looked like a choir.

I don't know what he'd thought we'd looked like before. But apparently not a choir.

The dresses came in the nick of time. At the crack of dawn on Friday—the day before the Spring Fling—the Clayton High Troubadours (along with Mr. Hall and select members of the Clayton High orchestra, who were accompanying us during our performance) were to board a specially hired bus. We would then travel to Bishop Luers High School, where we would face off with a dozen other show choirs. Each choir had fifteen minutes to dazzle the panel of highly prestigious judges—one was a former Miss Kentucky—with their vocal blend and balance, intonation, rhythmic precision, interpretation, tone quality, poise, appearance, pace of show, choreography, and overall performance skills.

I know. Could anything be more lame? I mean, a former Miss *Kentucky*? Hello, they at least could have gotten Andrew Lloyd Webber or somebody.

But you wouldn't believe how nervous everyone was about it, despite the lame quotient. Well, Mr. Hall and the sopranos were nervous, anyway. I have to confess, the altos seemed way more interested in seeing how many tiny pieces of paper we could make stick in Karen Sue Walters's curly hair as she stood on the riser beneath us.

Karen Sue accused of us throwing spit wads at her. Can

you believe it? And Mr. Hall blew the whole thing way out of proportion, if you ask me. They weren't spit wads at all, just little pieces of Bored Liz's trig homework.

Anyway, in the last week before we were to leave for Bishop Luers, Mr. Hall rehearsed us until "All that Jazz" seemed to play permanently in my head. We didn't have any problems with our vocal blend and balance, intonation, diction, or tone quality.

But according to Mr. Hall, some of us had a lot of problems with our rhythmic precision. And some of us—okay, well, one of us, anyway—had some major problems with the choreography.

My only defense is that when I'd auditioned, no one had ever said anything about dancing. Seriously. The part about singing I'd understood. But dancing? No one had said a word.

Ordinarily, of course, I'd have asked Trina to come over after school and help me out with the whole choreography thing. And ordinarily, she would have been happy to do so.

But Trina and I weren't speaking. Or rather, I was speaking to Trina.

The problem was, Trina wasn't speaking back.

This got old pretty fast. By Tuesday, I already thought it had gone on long enough.

And by Wednesday, I was way sick of it.

I was also sick of getting yelled at by Mr. Hall for screwing up the choreography. Which, if you think about it, was all Trina's fault, anyway. I mean, *she* was the one who'd been all, "Oh, it'll look good on your transcript."

Yeah, but what good was a nice-looking transcript if I happened to be DEAD? Because that's what I feared was going to happen if I didn't get Mr. Hall off my back about the stupid choreography. I was just going to fall down DEAD.

I was okay during "As Long as He Needs Me" (I'll Klingon Steadfastly) because it was a slow song. And since all we had to do for "Day by Day" was stand there in our stupid dresses and gaze into a spotlight—"You're looking into a beautiful sunset," Mr. Hall told us. "You're gazing at a rainbow, dazzled by the Lord's love!"—I was okay on that one, too.

But "All that Jazz." Oh, how I dreaded "All that Jazz." I could handle the step-ball-change during "I bought some aspirin down at United Drug." I could even handle the whole jazz hands things during "Start the car, I know a whoopee spot."

But when it came to getting Trina her freaking hat for the freaking kick line, I kept totally blowing it.

I'm just going to come right out and say that this, too, was Trina's fault. The week before, back when we'd still been speaking, I'd been throwing her the hat, and she'd been catching it and getting it on in time to get in place for the cancan.

But for some reason, even though I was throwing the hat in the exact same way, Trina kept missing it. I don't want to say on purpose. But . . .

All right. She was missing it on purpose.

The first couple of times this happened, Mr. Hall didn't notice, because the hat fell on the floor and Trina just scooped it up and put it on.

But during Wednesday's rehearsal—a particularly fractious one, because one of the tenors forgot his cummerbund, and I'd thought Mr. Hall was going to have an aneurism, he was so mad—Trina's hat flew out of my hand and landed, as luck would have it, inside Jake Mancini's tuba.

She could have caught it. She could have reached up and plucked it out of the air.

But she didn't. So it landed in the tuba.

Which was actually very funny, if you ask me. I mean, what were the chances? If it had happened during Luers, I was willing to bet Miss Kentucky would think we'd done it on purpose and given us extra points for aim and creativity.

It was no big deal. At least, I didn't think so. Jake removed the hat from his horn, handed it gallantly to Trina, and she put it on and got into the kick line without missing a single step.

Tough Brenda, who'd seen the whole thing, was laughing so hard—or so she told me later—she almost wet her tap pants (they came with the dress, on account of it having a very full skirt).

But Mr. Hall, who also saw the whole thing, did not seem to find it very amusing at all. His head whipped around, and he pinned me with a goggle-eyed look of pure, unadulterated rage. His face went as red as—well, as my dress.

When "All that Jazz" came to its rousing finish, and we were all standing there, our jazz hands stretched out, trying to exude as much poise and rhythmic precision as we were able, Mr. Hall threw down his baton and hissed, "Sit."

We all collapsed where we were, draped all over the risers.

Then Mr. Hall pointed at me.

"You," he growled. Really. Growled! "Stand."

I stood. My heart was beating fast. But only because I'd been doing jazz hands a few seconds before. I wasn't scared or anything. After all, it had been an accident. I hadn't done it on purpose. Surely Mr. Hall understood that.

Mr. Hall, it turned out, understood no such thing.

"Miss Greenley," Mr. Hall said. His face was still red, and there were large half moons of sweat under his armpits. He seemed oblivious to his own personal discomfort, though. All of his attention was focused on me.

"Is it your intention," he asked me, "to undermine and ruin this choir's performance while we are at Bishop Luers?"

I glanced down at Tough Brenda to see what she made of this question. I'd have looked to Trina for help, but she was keeping her face turned resolutely to the wall.

"Um," I said, since Tough Brenda's response was only an infinitesimal shrug, showing me that, as far as she knew, there was no right answer. "No?"

"Then why," Mr. Hall thundered, loudly enough to make the kid holding the cymbals almost drop them in his fright, "did you throw Catrina Larssen's hat into the orchestra pit during that last number?"

I looked at Steve, hoping for some backup on this one. None seemed forthcoming, at least from the baritone section. Steve's Adam's apple bobbed like a piston, but he didn't open his mouth.

"Um," I said finally. "It was an accident."

"AN ACCIDENT?" Mr. Hall screamed. "AN ACCIDENT? And do you know what that little ACCIDENT would have cost us if it had happened at Luers? DO YOU?"

Since I hadn't the foggiest idea, I said, "No."

"Ten points!" Mr. Hall roared. "Ten points, Miss Greenley, can mean the difference between first place and

NO PLACE. IS THAT WHAT YOU WANT, MISS GREEN-LEY? FOR THIS CHOIR NOT TO PLACE AT LUERS?"

I looked at Trina again. Had we been speaking, I knew that at this point, she would have raised her hand and said, *Mr. Hall, it was my fault, not Jen's. I should have caught the hat, but I didn't*, or something to that effect.

Except that if Trina and I had still been speaking, she wouldn't have let the hat fall into the tuba in the first place. So really, the whole thing was her fault.

Only I couldn't stand there and say that. *Mr. Hall, it wasn't my fault. It was Trina's.* Because you just don't *do* that.

So instead, I said, "I'm sorry, Mr. Hall. It won't happen again." Even though I knew it would. Because Trina was never going to catch that hat.

"Sorry isn't good enough," Mr. Hall yelled. "Sorry doesn't make it right! You have been sloughing off all year, Miss Greenley. It's like this choir is a big joke to you. Well, I will have you know that the Clayton High Troubadours are anything but a joke. We have won top honors at Bishop Luers for the past five years, and this year isn't going to be any different, despite your efforts to sabotage our perform-ance. I don't know if your little tryst with Luke Striker has gone to your head, missy, but allow me to assure you, *he's* the star. Not *you*. Now either you work with me, or you walk on out of here. The choice is yours."

Then Mr. Hall picked up his baton and rapped it on his conductor's stand.

"All right, people, let's take it from the top one more time," he said. "And let's hope that *this* time, Miss Greenley will show us a little more courtesy."

Here's the thing. Last week, I might have let it go. For Trina, because this was her thing, really. I was just along for the ride. She was the one with the big solo. She was the one who'd talked me into joining the stupid thing in the first place.

If this had been last week, I might have been all, *Okay, Mr. Hall. I apologize, Mr. Hall. I'll practice real hard to get it right, Mr. Hall.* Just to make things nice and easy for everybody.

But this wasn't last week.

And I didn't care about making things nice and easy for everybody.

I cared about making things right.

So I stepped down from the risers, walked around to where my street clothes were sitting—in a pile against the wall with my books—and scooped them up.

"Excuse me, Miss Greenley," Mr. Hall said. "Where do you think you're going?"

I looked over my shoulder at him as I made my way up the steps to the doors to the hallway.

"You told me to work with you or walk on out," I said. My heart was banging hard against my ribs. I had never sassed a teacher before. Never, not even once. But I didn't care what happened to me now. I told myself I didn't care a bit. "So I'm walking on out."

"Stop being so dramatic. Really, this is the kind of behavior I'd expect from Miss Larssen —" he glared at her darkly "—not *you*, Miss Greenley." He pointed to the empty space on the riser where I'd once stood. "Now get back to your place. Let's take it from the top, people."

"But." I stayed right where I was. "You said I had a choice."

"This is a *class*, Miss Greenley," Mr. Hall said. "You can't just leave in the middle of it."

Which is true. You can't just leave in the middle of class. Not without a hall pass. If you did, you could get detention, or worse, a suspension. Maybe you could even get expelled. How would I know? I'd never walked out in the middle of a class before. I'd always been a good kid. You know, the girl next door. The kind of girl who'd never quit anything in the middle and leave everybody in the lurch.

Mr. Hall knew that. Which was probably why he added, "You can't just *leave*."

And which might just be why I replied, "Watch me."

And walked away.

"Miss Greenley," I heard him scream. "Miss Greenley! Get back here this instant!"

But it was too late. I was already out of that choir room and heading down the hall, straight into the ladies' room, where I changed—my hands trembling—back into my normal clothes.

And you know what? Not a single person came after me to see if I was all right. No one asked Mr. Hall if it was okay to check on me. No one worried, the way I always had about Cara, that I might need a shoulder to cry on.

No one. No one at all.

Not even Trina, whose fault it all was in the first place.

Want to know why? Because the only person at Clayton High who'd ever cared enough to run after anyone to make sure she was okay was *me*.

Maybe that's why I took my dress—my hundred and eighty dollar, one hundred percent polyester Troubadours dress, with the sequined lightning bolt down the front—wadded it up, and threw it in the trash.

# Ask Annie

Ask Annie your most complex interpersonal relationship questions. Go on, we dare you! All letters to Annie are subject to publication in the Clayton High School *Register*. Names and e-mail addresses of correspondents guaranteed confidential.

Dear Annie,

Although I turned sixteen last week, my parents won't let me go out with boys, even on group dates. Recently a boy asked me go to the movies with him AND his parents, and my parents still said no.

Now my female friends don't want to hang out with me, because they know I'm not allowed to do anything where boys will be around. I'm dying of loneliness. What can I do?

Isolated in Indiana

Dear Isolated,

Tell your parents that you love them and you know they're trying to be protective, but they've gone too far. By preventing you from having a normal social life, they are not allowing you to learn to make decisions for yourself and develop healthy relationships, which will have a negative impact not just on your future ability to find a spouse but to function in a career and the world in general.

If they still refuse to listen, ask your pastor or a trusted teacher or other adult friend to intercede as an advocate. Good luck, and remember, as long as there's Annie, you'll never be alone.

Annie

# Thirteen

*I thought it* would take days before I'd be able to look back at what had happened in choir that day and laugh. Maybe even weeks. I mean, it had been pretty upsetting and all. I had defied a teacher, walked out on a bunch of people who were depending on me, and probably irrevocably severed ties with my best friend.

But it turned out it only took about three hours before the humorous side of the situation hit me. Because that's how long it was before the staff of the *Register* made me see it. The funny side, I mean.

Scott Bennett especially.

"You did *not*," he said, when I got to the part about stuffing my dress in the trash.

"No, I really did," I said.

I have to admit, the reaction of the paper's staff to the whole thing had given me confidence in myself and my decision. I had sat through the rest of my classes that afternoon expecting a summons from Juicy Lucy, who would undoubtedly call my parents, if she didn't just outright suspend me.

But no summons came from the vice principal's office. Nor did one come from Dr. Lewis's office. Or even Ms. Kellogg's. Mr. Hall apparently hadn't reported me.

Or more likely, he had, and no one from the office cared. Because it was, after all, *me*. And what kind of trouble was *Jen Greenley* likely to get up to, wandering the halls instead of sticking to her riser like a good little girl?

Scott and Geri and Kwang and the rest of the *Register*'s staff made me lighten up about it, though. They didn't know anything about Troubadours, really. Except that Kwang had been going to join them on the bus to Luers, to cover the event for the paper. Since the Clayton High sports teams lose every game they play, people were putting a lot of stock into the Troubadours pulling through for the Roosters.

"Now who'm I gonna sit by?" Kwang asked with a groan, since without me there, he'd have no one to joke around with on the bus.

"There's Trina," I pointed out. "And Steve."

"Theater types," Kwang said disgustedly.

"I can't believe you just threw it away," Scott said, still referring to my dress. This was the part he couldn't seem to wrap his mind around. That I'd thrown away my dress.

And I guess it *was* pretty weird. I mean, considering it had been kind of expensive.

But that had been the point. I had paid for that stupid dress with my own money. Baby-sitting money. Money I could have spent on . . . I don't know. But something I actually liked.

"What do you think I should have done with it?" I shook my head. "I mean, it's not like I was ever going to wear it again."

"Yeah, Scott," Geri said. They had reached a point in their new, unromantic relationship where they could tease each other again. I wasn't quite sure if this was a good sign or a bad one. But I was relieved that neither of them seemed to be pining for the other. In fact, lately, Geri seemed to have been in a pretty good mood. "What, you think there're a lot of places where a girl can wear a red dress with a lightning bolt down the front?"

"Yeah," Kwang said. "You think she should maybe wear it to the Spring Fling with Luke Striker?"

Everyone laughed *really* hard at that one.

Then Geri suggested we go back to the ladies' room where I'd dumped the dress, fish it out of the trash can, and have a ceremonial burning and/or burying of it. Scott had a better idea, though: We should pour chemicals from the darkroom on it—since it was made of so many unnatural fibers—and see if we could make the dress explode.

I felt weird about going so near the choir room so soon after what had happened—I didn't want to run into Mr. Hall or Trina or anybody—so I declined to go on the "recon mission" to collect the dress. Instead, Geri went with a couple of the freshmen girls. They came back empty-handed, though. The custodians had already taken out the trash.

This led to a lot of jokes about what if one of the custodians found the dress and decided to keep it, and the hilarity that might ensue if we happened to catch one of them wearing it. You know, beneath his coveralls.

It was stupid, I know. But I swear I almost wet my pants, I was laughing so hard.

Which was why, after the meeting was over, I didn't hear Scott say my name. Because I was still laughing too hard.

"I'll give you a ride home if you need one, Jen," Scott said.

I swear, he said it so casually that at first I didn't quite realize the enormity of the situation. You know, because he says it every day, practically. I just went—remembering that Trina wasn't speaking to me and that I wouldn't be able to count on a ride from Steve anyway, since they were broken up—"Oh, cool, thanks."

I got my backpack and followed Scott through the long, empty hallways to the student parking lot. We chatted casually along the way. Scott said he'd heard Avril Lavigne couldn't ride a skateboard to save her life, and didn't that make her a big phony; and I defended her, saying that she'd never professed to be a skateboarder herself, just that she hung out with skateboarders.

This naturally led to a discussion of the merits of skateboarding, and if we were rebuilding civilization, like in *Lucifer's Hammer*, would we let skateboarders into our new utopian society (Scott: Absolutely not. Skateboarding is not a useful skill. Me: Maybe. Because skateboarders often understand things like physics. They have to, while building those half pipes and all).

It was just so . . . *easy*. Walking down the hall and talking to Scott, I mean. Like we'd been doing it our whole lives.

Except that we hadn't. There'd always been a third person along. I just didn't happen to notice—then—that she was missing.

It was still a beautiful spring afternoon when we got outside. The sky was like this big blue overturned salad bowl in the sky. It was hard to believe there were planets and stars and stuff spinning around behind it. In fact, in the old days that's what people used to think—that the sky was like this huge colander over the Earth and that the stars were the light from heaven, shining through pinpricks in the protective covering of sky. People were all scared of the sky cracking and letting in the full force of the light of heaven, which they thought would kill us all. . . .

I was mentioning this to Scott as we got to his car and he was opening the passenger door for me. It wasn't until I found myself staring down at the passenger seat—the empty passenger seat, the one in the front—that it hit me: Geri Lynn wasn't with us. Geri Lynn wasn't with us, because Scott and Geri Lynn had broken up. Scott and I were alone with each other.

Scott and I were alone with each other for the first time *ever*.

I don't know why that realization made me feel so . . . weird. I mean, Scott and I talk *all* the time, at lunch and at the *Register* meetings.

But the truth is, there are always other people around then. And, okay, maybe they aren't taking part in our conversation. But they're still *there*.

Being alone with him like this . . .

Well, it was just *weird*.

Like the front seat thing, for example. I'd never sat in the front seat of Scott's car before. Ever. I'd always been in the back, behind Geri Lynn. All I'd been able to see from back there, as a matter of fact, was Geri's big blond aurora of hair.

But from the front seat, it turned out, I could see all this stuff I'd never noticed before. Like Scott's CD collection, for instance, which included so many artists that I also had in my own . . . Ms. Dynamite and Bree Sharp and Garbage and Jewel.

And the fuzzy dice hanging from his rearview mirror with SEE RUBY FALLS printed on them.

And Scott's hand on the gearshift, just inches from my thigh. Scott's big strong hand, the one that had lifted me up, up, up toward that stupid log. . . .

I think I would have been all right. I think I would have been able to handle the weirdness of being alone with Scott in the front seat of his car if—*wham*—the memory of all those times Trina had said I should have asked Scott out hadn't came flooding back. *You're perfect for each other,* Trina's voice was suddenly saying, over and over, in my head. *Why don't you ask him out?*

*Shut up, Trina,* I said right back at her. But, you know, inside my head. *Shut up!*

It was amazing to me how my ex–best friend could ruin even a perfectly innocent thing like a car ride . . . and without even being there!

I don't know if Scott noticed how I'd suddenly fallen silent. I don't see how he couldn't. I mean, normally we talk a mile a minute to each other.

But, I swear, once I heard Trina's voice in my head, telling me I should have asked Scott out, I couldn't think of a single other thing.

Except for maybe all of those hearts in Geri Lynn's date book. Those I couldn't get out of my mind, for some reason.

Scott didn't seem to mind my sudden muteness. In fact, he took advantage of it to say, as we turned down my street, "Can I ask you a question, Jen?"

What could be less threatening? He wanted to ask me a question. That was all. Just a question.

So why did my heart start to pound so hard inside my chest? Why did my palms suddenly feel all sweaty? So why was I having trouble breathing?

"Shoot," I managed to wheeze at him.

Only I never did get to find out what Scott wanted to ask me, because we had pulled up in front of my house . . .

. . . and seven or eight reporters rushed at the car, each of them shouting questions of their own at me.

"Jen, Jen," one of them was crying. "What color will you be wearing to the prom? Can you just give us a hint?"

"Miss Greenley," another one shouted. "Hair up? Or hair down? Teens want to know!"

"Jen," shrieked a third. "Will you be going with Luke to Toronto, where he'll be filming his next project?"

"God," Scott said, about the reporters. "They're still hounding you?"

"Pretty much," I said. And took a deep breath, trying to

slow down my still wildly beating heart. "What was it you wanted to ask me, Scott?"

"Oh," Scott said. "Nothing." Then he grinned and, pretending he was holding a microphone, pointed it into my face. "What does it feel like to be the envy of millions of girls across the country, Miss Greenley?"

"No comment," I said, with a relieved smile. Joking. He was joking around with me. So it was all right . . .

. . . whatever *it* was.

Then I jumped out of the car and into the cluster of reporters.

"See you tomorrow!" I called to Scott.

"See you," Scott said.

But even then—even though the two of us had separated and weren't alone with each other anymore—things were still weird. Because I noticed that Scott waited until I got past the reporters—"Jenny, Jenny, what's it like knowing you're going to the spring formal with the winner of the People's Choice Award for Sexiest New Star?"—and had the door open and everything before he pulled away. He wanted to make sure I got in all right, even though it was, you know, broad daylight and all.

What did that mean? I mean, seriously?

And it occurred to me that, now that Scott and Geri were broken up, I could have gotten online and written to Trina about it. You know, have been all, *Ohmygod, just now when Scott dropped me off, he waited to make sure I got in all right before he pulled away. What do you think that means?* Because, you know, Scott wasn't taken anymore.

Only I couldn't write that to Trina. Because we still weren't speaking.

And also because it would have just been too weird. Because I don't think of Scott that way.

Do I?

*Should* I?

Only I didn't really have time to think about it, because the minute I walked through the door, the phone started ringing.

At first I'd been almost sure it was her. Trina, I mean. Calling to say how sorry she was about what had happened in choir that day, and asking me to forgive her.

Except that it wasn't Trina. It turned out to be Karen Sue Walters.

I couldn't imagine what Karen Sue wanted—she'd never called me at home before.

What Karen Sue wanted, it turned out, was to make sure I was all right. She joked about Mr. Hall's temper, saying, "We theater types. We just can't help it." Then she said she hoped she'd see me tomorrow in rehearsal.

"I don't think so," I said slowly, wondering what was

going on. I mean, it was kind of weird that Karen Sue was wondering if I was all right *now*, hours after the fact. I hadn't noticed that she'd been so concerned earlier in the day, when it had all actually happened.

"I don't think I'm cut out for the whole show choir thing," I told her. "You said it yourself . . . theater types. I'm just not one of them."

Karen Sue's voice got different then. She asked me if I realized how much I was letting everyone down. Not just her and the choir but the whole school. The whole school was depending on the Troubadours to win for them at Bishop Luers.

That's when I realized why Karen Sue had really called. Not because she cared about my mental health or anything. Obviously, since she hadn't run after me when I'd left the choir room that day.

But because they hadn't found anybody else to give Trina her hat.

So I told Karen Sue that the only way she'd see me at rehearsal the next day was if someone dragged my cold life-less carcass onto the risers and left it there.

Then I hung up before I could apologize for saying it.

Karen Sue wasn't the only person from Troubadours who called that evening. I heard from a bunch of other sopranos. Not Trina, of course. Not the person who should have called me, whose fault the whole thing was. But a few of the others.

But I told them all the same thing I'd told Karen Sue: No, I was not coming back to show choir.

When the phone rang at eleven that night, my dad—who, like my mom, had no idea what was going on . . . and I preferred to keep it that way—grumbled, "And I thought it was bad back when you and Trina were still speaking. . . ."

But when I picked up the phone, it wasn't another Troubadour, begging me to come back to the fold.

It was Luke Striker.

"Jen," he said. "Hey. Hope I didn't wake you up. It's only nine out here in L.A. I forgot about the time difference. Are your parents mad?"

They were, of course, but not at Luke. I assured him it was all right. And then I wondered why he was calling. Was he, I asked myself, calling to cancel on me? About the Spring Fling, I mean.

I know it sounds crazy. I know any other girl in America would have been dreading a call like this. You know, Luke Striker canceling a date with them.

But me? I was trying to ignore my leaping pulse. Because if Luke canceled on me, I'd be free . . . free to go to Kwang's anti–Spring Fling party. Free to hang out there.

I didn't ask myself why this thought should be so appealing. I didn't ask myself who it was I wanted to hang out *with* at Kwang's party.

And I didn't ask myself if maybe this had something to do with the question a certain person had wanted to ask me earlier in the evening. . . .

*OhpleasecancelSpringFling. PleasepleasecancelSpringFling. ComeonLukecancelSpringFlingwithme.* . . .

But that wasn't why Luke was calling me. That wasn't why he was calling me at all.

"I heard what happened today," he said. "In choir."

I nearly dropped the phone.

"You *did?* How did *you* hear about it? Who told you? Was it Ms. Kellogg? My God, she doesn't know, does she?"

"It wasn't Ms. Kellogg," Luke said with a chuckle. "Let's just say I have my sources."

Sources? What sources? What was he talking about?

"Oh my God," I said, feeling cold hard fear grip me. "Was it on the news? About my quitting show choir?" Who had told? Who could have told? And how dead was I going to be when my parents found out?

"Relax," Luke said. Now he was outright laughing. "It wasn't on the news. I wish it had been, though. I wish I could have been there to see that hat fly into the tuba. . . ."

"It's not funny," I said, even though just a few hours before I'd been cracking up laughing over it. "Well, not *that* funny, anyway. Everybody's mad at me. Luke, I've never had so many people mad at me before."

"Good," Luke said. "That means it's working."

"What's working?"

"What we talked about," he said. "You can't effect social change, Jen, without ruffling a few feathers."

"Oh," I said. "Well, I wouldn't exactly call my quitting choir effecting social change."

"Oh, it is," Luke said. "Maybe not as much as what you did for Cara, but—"

"Wait," I said. "How do *you* know what happened with Cara?"

"I told you," Luke said with a laugh. "I have my sources."

I wondered who on earth Luke could have been talking to. Since his "outing" in Clayton, he'd fled back to his Hollywood Hills mansion, where Pat O'Brien and people like that said he was "in seclusion," still refusing to speak to the press about Angelique's dumping him and his subsequent—one reporter called it "zany"—decision to attend high school undercover in a small, rural Midwestern town. Everyone, it seemed, wanted to know what was going on with Luke Striker and what they called his "bizarre" behavior.

But really, I didn't think Luke's wanting to be alone—or even to go to high school—was so bizarre. It wasn't as if he were climbing up trees and declaring himself to be Peter Pan, like *some* celebrities.

"Listen, Jen," he said, in that soft deep voice that had made him such a convincing Lancelot. You could so totally see why Guenevere would go for him instead of the other guy, the one who'd played King Arthur. "I just wanted to call and say how proud I am of you. You're doing great. How are things going on the Betty Ann front?"

Betty Ann! Oh, Lord, I'd completely forgotten about Betty Ann.

"I'm, uh, working on it," I lied.

"Great," Luke said. "So I'll see you Saturday, all right? And Jen?"

"Yeah?"

"I knew you could do it."

I thanked him and hung up. But I didn't exactly share his enthusiasm. I mean, what, exactly, had I done? I'd alienated my best friend. I'd quit show choir right before their big crucial performance—a real team player, that's me. I'd have to skip fourth period choir tomorrow, which meant I'd probably get caught and consequently suspended.

And now I was going to have to go up against the most popular guy in school to get my favorite teacher's Cabbage Patch doll back.

Oh, yeah. Things were going great.

# Ask Annie

**Ask Annie your most complex interpersonal relationship questions. Go on, we dare you! All letters to Annie are subject to publication in the Clayton High School *Register*. Names and e-mail addresses of correspondents guaranteed confidential.**

Dear Annie,

There's a guy that I like as more than just a friend, but he seems to think we're only buddies. He asks for my advice on girls, and has gone out with all my friends but never me. It just kills me! Should I come out and tell him I like him? What if that makes things weird between us, and he doesn't even want to be my friend anymore? I wouldn't be able to stand it if we weren't friends. Help! What should I do?

> Tired of Sitting Home While He's Out with Other Girls

Dear Tired,

I have news for you: The two of you aren't friends now. You can't be friends with someone you have a crush on. You have a choice:

either decide that as a couple, the two of you aren't meant to be, or ask him point-blank why he's asked out everyone you know except for you. Either he'll mumble something incoherent (in which case you'll know he's not attracted to you) or he'll say, "I never knew you were interested!" and ask you. Either way, you'll have your answer.

Annie

*Fourteen*

*Operation Return of* Betty Ann went into action the very next morning. And not a minute too soon, either: Kurt and his friends had sent Mrs. Mulvaney another ransom note. This one was even lamer than the last one. This one said, *If U don't give EVERY1 in your classes an A for the semester, Betty Ann's head goes in the disposal.*

Mrs. Mulvaney actually went pale as she read the note—which she'd found folded on her desk where Betty Ann used to sit—aloud to us. Her fingers shook as she held it.

She didn't say anything more about it after that—just crumpled it up and threw it away.

But I knew. I knew they'd gone too far. The abduction of Betty Ann had gone from a kind of funny prank to an outright act of cruelty.

And I wasn't going to let it go on a second longer.

My plan went into action during fourth period, when I

should have been in show choir. Only when the bell rang, instead of going to class, I ducked into the guidance office and went up to Mrs. Templeton, Ms. Kellogg's administrative assistant.

"Well, hello, Jenny," Mrs. Templeton said. "Do you have an appointment with Ms. Kellogg right now? Because I didn't see your name on her calendar."

"I don't have an appointment," I said. "Actually, you're the one I need to talk to."

Mrs. Templeton looked pleasantly surprised. "*Me?* Well, I can't imagine what *I* could do for you, Jenny. . . ."

"It's kind of embarrassing, actually," I said, lowering my voice, as if I were afraid other people in the office might overhear. "I'm hoping we could just keep it between ourselves. Can you— Can I trust you to keep a secret, Mrs. T.?"

Mrs. Templeton—who loves gossip more than any other human being I know, and has probably never kept a secret in her life, which is why Ms. Kellogg asked me to never reveal to Mrs. T. that I'm Ask Annie—leaned forward.

"Of course you can," she whispered.

So then I told her.

Oh, not the truth, of course . . . I mean, that I was skipping show choir because I'd walked out and had no intention of returning. Or that I'm Ask Annie. Or that I had a bad feeling I might be attracted to Scott Bennett.

What I told her instead was how, due to the stress of being Luke Striker's date for the Spring Fling and having *Entertainment Tonight* trailing me around and all, I had forgotten my locker combination.

Just flat out forgotten it.

"Is that all?" Mrs. T. looked disappointed. "Well, we can take care of that in a jiffy, hon, don't you worry."

And then, as I'd known she would, Mrs. Templeton lugged out this huge binder in which was recorded the combination of every locker in the school.

"What's your locker number again, hon?" Mrs. Templeton asked me.

"Three forty-five," I told her, blithely giving her not my own locker number but Kurt Schraeder's.

Mrs. Templeton didn't know what locker number I had. She had no way of knowing I was outright lying to her. She said, "Well, isn't your combo twenty-one, thirty-five, twenty-eight?"

I quickly jotted the numbers down. "Yeah," I said, looking at them with a funny expression on my face. "Wow. Of course. How weird that I'd forget."

"Well," Mrs. Templeton said sympathetically, "you've been through a lot, hon. I mean, that Luke Striker . . . why, if I'd been hanging around with him as much as you have, I'd forget everything I used to know, too . . . especially the fact that I'm married!"

I laughed very hard at Mrs. Templeton's little joke.

"Good one," I said. "Well, I'm just going to go get my books now. So I can get to class."

"Sure thing, hon," Mrs. Templeton said. "Oh, here, let me write you a pass so you don't get into trouble. . . ."

It was that easy.

I hurried down the empty hall, listening to the drone of teachers' voices behind each door I passed. *"Alyx mis du sel dans le bol du Michel. . . ." "If* x *goes into* y *five times, then* y *must be . . ." "And Congress said, 'Well, each time we have an election, we can't have a murder,' so Alexander Hamilton . . ."*

Finally, I reached locker number three forty-five. I gave the combination lock a whirl, then went to work.

Left, twenty-one.

Right all the way around, thirty-five.

Look up and down the hallway, make sure no one's coming. Especially Kurt Schraeder.

Then a few notches back to the left, twenty-eight. . . .

The locker door popped open.

Nothing.

Oh, plenty of raunchy magazines, textbooks, stickers that said GO ROOSTERS! and BLINK 182 SUX. A letter jacket. A box of Trojans (nice). And an extremely pungent and not very appealing odor.

But no Betty Ann. No Betty Ann at all.

Crushed—but not defeated—I closed the locker and slunk down to the library, where I hid until the bell rang for lunch. I never even had to show the librarian my pass. She didn't even ask what I was doing in there instead of in class. Because, you know. I'm nice little Jenny Greenley.

I tell you, I'm starting to think there might actually be advantages to this girl-next-door thing.

When the bell finally rang, I was one of the first people in the caf.

And when Kurt and his friends sauntered in, I made a beeline for him.

"Jen?" Cara called after me, as I tore from the table where we'd been sitting. "Where are you going?"

"I'll be right back," I said. I hurried down the catwalk to where Kurt was standing in the lunch line, trying to decide between sausage and peppers or a turkey burger.

"Kurt," I said to him. "Where's Betty Ann?"

Kurt looked down at me. "What? Oh, it's you again. What is with you and that stupid doll?"

"Where is she, Kurt?"

"Relax," Kurt said. "She's in a safe place."

"Where is she, Kurt?"

Kurt looked from me to his buddies, then gave one of his asinine little laughs. "What is with you?" he asked me again.

"Why are you always raggin' on me? First the Cara Cow thing, now this. Jesus, we're just trying to have a little fun."

"Just tell me if the doll's all right, will you?" I asked.

"She's fine," Kurt said. "She's in my room somewhere, okay? Now will you stop worrying about stuff that doesn't concern you, and let me order my lunch? Or are you just gonna stand there?"

I got out of his way and went back down the catwalk to my seat.

"What was *that* all about?" Geri Lynn wanted to know as I sat down.

"Nothing," I said. I dug into my tuna salad sandwich, only to see Scott's gaze on me. When my glance met his, however, he looked away.

Suddenly, I wasn't hungry anymore.

I was sitting there peacefully, wondering at my sudden lack of appetite—I'd been totally ravenous before—while Cara and Kwang took part in a spirited debate about the merit of the Rose McGowan episodes versus the Shannen Doherty years of *Charmed* when I felt a tap on my shoulder. I turned around to see Karen Sue Walters standing there, with about half of the sopranos—though not Trina, I noticed—from Troubadours behind her.

What on earth were they doing out of the choir room?

"We just want to say thanks," Karen Sue said in a very

high-pitched, sarcastic voice, "for letting down the choir. We'll be thinking about you tomorrow when we place first at Luers."

I looked over at Steve to see if he'd known anything in advance about this little noontime ambush of me. But he looked as bewildered as I felt.

I turned back toward Karen Sue to say, *You're welcome*, the only conceivable response to such a statement, but I didn't get a chance to.

That's because Cara Schlosburg suddenly pushed back her chair and stood up.

Can I just say that, busty as Karen Sue might have been, she could not hold a candle to Cara?

"Why don't you guys just leave her alone?" Cara demanded of Karen Sue and her friends. "Don't you think she's been through enough without you guys trying to make her feel worse?"

Karen Sue was so flabbergasted that for a few seconds she could only blink up at Cara, completely taken aback. Then she seemed to recover herself, since she tittered and said, "Oh, right! Like I really care what *you* think, Cara Cow."

If she'd said, *Hey! I found a winning lottery ticket!* the silence that roared through the caf following this statement could not have been more profound. Everyone seemed to stop what they were doing and look over at our table. Our table, which for years had been an oasis of peace in a sea of unrest and intimidation.

I don't know what they were expecting. I mean, for me to do. Launch myself at Karen Sue, fingernails first? A little catfight in the caf for their lunchtime entertainment?

Well, they were destined for disappointment.

I couldn't help sighing a little. Really, had Luke had any idea—when he'd given me his little speech about how it was up to people like me to effect social change—how very, very hard accomplishing such tasks could be? It was a project with absolutely no conceivable end in sight.

I was about to tell Karen Sue exactly what I thought of her of stooping to the level of the Kurts of the world, when again I was interrupted.

But this time, it was by Scott Bennett.

"You know what," he said, putting down his napkin and speaking in a world-weary voice, "this is really starting to piss me off. We were just sitting here, enjoying a nice meal, and you girls had to come ruin it."

"It's a free country," Karen Sue started to insist shrilly.

But Kwang—all two hundred fifty pounds of him—scooted his chair back and stood up.

"You heard the man," he said. "Get out of here."

The sopranos, their eyes going as wide as snickerdoodles,

scattered like rabbits, running off in all different directions.

And everyone in the room went back to what they'd been doing before the girls had tried their stupid stunt.

Well, everyone except for me. Because my heart was too full of appreciation for what my friends—my *real* friends—had done for me.

"You guys," I said, feeling tears prick the corners of my eyes. "You guys, that was so sweet—"

"Oh my God," Kwang said, looking at me in horror. "You aren't going to cry, are you?"

"Of course she isn't," Geri Lynn said, passing me a tissue. "Don't you start crying, Jen. You'll make *me* start crying. And I'm not wearing waterproof mascara today."

That made me laugh. My eyes were so filled with tears, I couldn't see my tuna fish sandwich. But I was still laughing.

"Why'd you ever join that stupid choir in the first place?" Scott asked me in the car on our way home from that day's *Register* meeting. I hadn't been too surprised when he'd offered me another ride.

Scared. But not surprised.

But I wasn't scared for the reasons you might think. I mean, it wasn't like I thought Scott was going to make any huge declaration of love for me in his Audi or anything. What had happened at lunch that day had been great in one way but not so great in another. And the not so great way was Scott's standing up for me—or, really, Cara—like that.

It meant he really and truly did consider me his friend.

And the problem with Scott considering me his friend?

He probably didn't consider me much more than that.

I mean, think about it. I consider Luke my friend. In no way would I ever want to date him. Luke, I mean.

So Scott thinking of me as a friend? Not such a good thing.

Because I was sort of getting the feeling—from the losing my appetite at lunch thing and the sweaty palms I'd experienced in his car the day before—that maybe I kind of liked him as more than just a friend.

I blamed Trina for this, just like I blamed her for the whole Troubadours thing. Because if she hadn't put the idea in my head all those months ago, it might never have occurred to me, now that Scott and Geri Lynn had broken up and he was available, that I might . . . that he might . . . that *we* might . . .

Oh, God. Just forget it. Because it wasn't going to happen. So why bother thinking about it? Because even if I *were* starting to think of him as more than just a friend, he obviously still thought of me as nice little Jenny Greenley, Ask Annie, everybody's best friend.

Which is fine. It's good, actually. It means it's okay for

me to accept rides home from school with him. So that's nice.

So what was I feeling scared about as I rode home with him?

What I knew was going to happen next.

"Hey, listen," I said, as the sign for Sycamore Hills, the street where Kurt Schraeder lived—at least according to the phone book, which listed only one Schraeder residence, Kurt Schraeder, Sr. "Can we make a little detour?"

"Sure," Scott said. "Where to?"

"Turn here," I said. "At the sign."

Scott turned, and soon we were cruising down a nice street—not far from where Cara lived, actually—dotted by largish, slightly-on-the-new-side houses.

"Are you going to fill me in on what we're doing here?" Scott asked above the dulcet tones of Aimee Mann on his car stereo.

"We're about to stage a rescue," I said mysteriously.

"A rescue? Of what? A dentist?" He was referring to the suburbany architecture, which I'm proud to say my dad had had nothing to do with.

"No," I said. "Of Betty Ann Mulvaney."

"Whoa," Scott said, looking impressed. "What are you going to do? Break in and take her? Shouldn't we wait until dark? Hey, I think Kwang's got some night-vision goggles. . . ."

"Very funny. But we don't need night-vision goggles," I told him. "Or the cover of darkness."

Kurt's house—which was number 1532 Sycamore Hills—came up on our right. It was an impressive Tudor job. Kurt's Grand Am, I was pleased to see, was not in the driveway.

"So," Scott said, as he pulled into the driveway and switched the ignition off. "What now?"

"Watch and learn, my friend," I said, undoing my seat belt. "Watch and learn."

Scott followed me up the steps to the Schraeders' front door. I rang the bell.

Look, I won't lie to you. The watch-and-learn bit? An act. A total act. I guess I'm more of a theater type than I ever imagined.

The truth was, I was totally nervous. My stomach hurt. My heart was racing a mile a minute. My hands were all sweaty—not because of Scott this time, but because I had no idea whether or not my plan was going to work.

But, hey, I knew one thing: If I didn't even try, no *way* was it going to.

The door was opened—as I'd hoped it would be—by Kurt's little sister. Her name, I knew from her necklace, was Vicky. I dropped my hands down to my knees (which was good, because then I could wipe the sweat off on my jeans) so that my gaze was level with hers and said, "Hi! Do you know me?"

Vicky pulled the braid tip she'd been sucking on out of her mouth and went, with a stunned expression, "Oh my Gosh! You're Jenny Greenley! You're the one going to the Spring Fling with *Luke Striker*! I saw you on *MTV News*!"

"Yes, that's me," I said modestly. "Is your brother Kurt home?"

Vicky shook her head, her eyes big as jawbreakers. "No. He went to the lake. With Courtney."

"Oh, no," I said, trying to look disappointed. The acting thing was getting easier and easier. "Well, did he leave something for me? A doll?"

Vicky's eyes grew even wider. "You mean Betty Ann?"

"Yes," I said, my stomach starting to hurt less. "Betty Ann. See, it's my turn to look after her. Betty Ann, I mean. I guess Kurt forgot. Could you do me a favor? Could you run to his room and get her for me?"

Back went the tip of the braid into the mouth.

"I'm not allowed to go in Kurt's room," Vicky said, as she sucked energetically. "He said if I did it again, he'd tell Mom on me."

"Oh, he won't mind this one time, Vicky," I said. "In fact, you'll be doing him a huge favor. Because, you see, if I don't get Betty Ann back—and right this very minute—someone is going to go to the school principal and tell him that Kurt's the one who took Betty Ann in the first place, and then Kurt probably won't get to graduate."

The braid dropped from Vicky's mouth. "Someone would *do* that?"

"Oh, yes," I said, elbowing Scott, who'd begun to chuckle. "*Someone* would. So, you see, you'd really be helping Kurt if you could do this one little thing for me."

"Okay," Vicky said with a shrug. "I'll be right back."

She took off. When I glanced at Scott, he was shaking his head at me.

"What *happened* to you?" he wanted to know.

"What do you mean?" I asked, a little alarmed.

"You never used to be like this," Scott said. "You used to . . . I don't know. Be much more interested in smoothing things over than in stirring things up."

I couldn't believe he'd noticed. I mean, that he'd been paying attention.

To *me*.

"I don't know," I said, looking away so he wouldn't see that I was blushing. "I guess I just decided to take a stand."

"I'll say," Scott said.

We heard running footsteps, and then Vicky reappeared, Betty Ann in her arms.

Betty Ann did not look well. Her yarn hair was a little on

the bedraggled side, and there appeared to be barbecue sauce on her overalls.

But she was in one piece. Her head had not been put down any disposals. She was still recognizably Betty Ann Mulvaney.

"Here she is," Vicky said, handing the doll over. "I found her under Kurt's bed."

"Thanks, Vicky," I said, tucking Betty Ann beneath my arm. "You're the best."

"And listen," Scott said to Vicky. "When Kurt comes home, will you tell him what happened? Tell him Scott Bennett came by and said if you didn't give him the doll, someone would go to the principal and tell on him."

"No. Jenny Greenley," I said quickly, giving Scott a *what-do-you-think-you're-doing?* look.

"No," Scott said, giving me the look right back. "Scott Bennett."

"I'll tell him you both came over," Vicky said, "if you think you could get me Luke Striker's autograph. Could you do that, Jenny? Pleeeeease?"

"Sure thing," I said, and waved as we hurried down the steps to Scott's car.

"Why'd you do that?" I asked him, as soon as we were safely on the road again. "Tell her your name like that?"

"Because when Kurt finds out what you did," Scott said,

"he's going to go ballistic. And if he's going to pound anyone's face in, I think it should at least be someone who's in a position to pound him back."

Suddenly I was blinking back tears again. I couldn't believe it. Twice in one day, he'd come galloping to my rescue like . . .

Well, like Lancelot.

"Oh, great," Scott said. "You aren't crying again, are you?"

"No," I said with a sniffle.

I couldn't help it, though. The fact that he was willing to sacrifice his own face in order to keep mine from getting bashed in? It was really the nicest thing anyone had ever done for me. It *had* to mean he thought of me as more than just a friend, didn't it?

I mean, didn't it?

We'd pulled up to a stop sign. Suddenly, Scott's hand left the gearshift, and he leaned toward me . . .

I'll admit it. My heart leaped. My pulse staggered. I thought he was going to kiss me. I thought he was going to lean in close, cup my tearstained cheeks in his hands, and whisper, *Please don't cry, Jenny,* and kiss me.

I know! I don't know where it came from! But, suddenly, it was there, in my head.

My heart started thrumming in my chest way louder

than the kettledrum back at Troubadour rehearsals had ever sounded, and my breath caught in my throat. . . .

But instead of reaching over to cup my face in his hands, Scott leaned over to pop open the glove box. He reached inside, took something out, and handed it to me.

And, no, it was not his class ring or anything like that.

It was a wad of Dairy Queen napkins.

"You're gonna get the doll wet," was all he said.

# Ask Annie

Ask Annie your most complex interpersonal relationship
questions. Go on, we dare you! All letters to Annie are subject
to publication in the Clayton High School *Register.* Names and
e-mail addresses of correspondents guaranteed confidential.

Dear Annie,

It's almost the end of school, and I want to
spend my summer like the rest of the kids I
know—going to the lake, hanging out at the
mall, and, you know, just chilling. I figure
after nine months of studying my butt off, I
deserve a little R and R.

The problem is my parents. They insist
that I get a job. They say I have to start
earning money for college. But isn't it their
job to pay for college? Can you please print
this letter, because I know my parents'll do
whatever you say, because they think, like I
do, that you're the bomb.

Catching Rays

Dear Rays,

I may not be the bomb, but I'm definitely

going to drop one: Your parents are right. Nobody "deserves" three months off. Do your parents, who probably work as hard all year long as you've studied, get three months off? No.

Take two weeks. Then get a job. And go to the lake or hang out at the mall on weekends. The money will come in handy someday. And so will the references.

Annie

## Fifteen

*Betty Ann Mulvaney* was back in her place of honor on Mrs. Mulvaney's desk the next morning.

My mom had done what she could to clean her up. She'd managed to get the barbecue sauce out of Betty Ann's overalls, and we both spent an hour trying to straighten out the mess her yarn hair had gotten into. We'd finally ended up twisting it into two braids, and fastening them with some ribbon my mom had left over from a country-style kitchen she'd done.

The result was that although Betty Ann did not look *exactly* like she had before her ordeal, she at least looked . . . okay.

And when Mrs. Mulvaney walked in and saw her . . .

Well, you could tell she didn't think there was anything wrong with Betty Ann at all.

*"Betty Ann!"* Mrs. Mulvaney said with a gasp. I don't

think Mrs. M. even noticed that I'd been standing beside the doll, keeping watch over her. After all the trouble I'd gone to to get her back, no way was I going to let Kurt steal her again.

Scott's assumption—that the two of us were going to get our faces pounded in for what we'd done—turned out to be erroneous. It looked as if Vicky had managed to convey the most important part of my message to Kurt—the part about not getting his diploma if "someone" happened to spill the truth behind Betty Ann's kidnapping to Dr. Lewis.

Consequently, Kurt didn't utter a word as he came into the Latin room that morning and sank into his desk. He glared at me, all right, standing up by Mrs. M.'s desk, one eye on the door and the other on Betty Ann.

But that's all he did.

By the end of the class period, when Kurt merely strolled past me and out of the room without so much as a glance, I was convinced that Luke had been 100 percent right: I *do* have more power than I'd ever known.

Way more power, as I found out when fourth period rolled around.

But back to Mrs. M. Was there an immediate and sustained change in her demeanor upon finding Betty Ann returned to her safe and—except for the braids—mostly sound?

You bet there was. The woman was practically giddy with

relief. I know it sounds dumb—that someone could love a doll so much—but Mrs. Mulvaney was like a changed person. She didn't ask where Betty Ann had been. She didn't thank us for her return.

Instead, she just started having fun with us again, teaching us phrases that would be way more useful for a frat party—if you could find one where everyone spoke Latin—than the SATs. Phrases like:

*Bibat ille, bibat illa,*
*bibat servus et ancilla,*
*bibat hera, bibat herus,*
*ad bibendum nemo serus!*

Which means, basically, everybody get drunk now.

I know! Shocking!

But not as shocking as what happened a few periods later.

It was Friday. The bus the school had hired to take the Troubadours to Luers had left at six in the morning, and wasn't due to return until after dark, if the Troubadours made the finals. Was I relieved to know I'd have one day, anyway, safe from worrying about bumping into Mr. Hall or Karen Sue? Yes.

Was I worried that my time was running out and that,

sooner or later, I was going to get busted for having skipped my fourth period class three days in a row?

Totally. I couldn't believe I hadn't been called in to see Ms. Kellogg about it yet. Mr. Hall had to have marked me as absent from his class yesterday. Did Ms. K. think it was a mistake or something? I mean, nice little Jenny Greenley would *never* skip a class.

Well, she'd find out it hadn't been a mistake soon enough, I supposed.

Anyway, when fourth period rolled around that day, I was in the library—where else did I have to go?—quietly going over my trig homework, when someone suddenly sank down into the study carrel next to mine and said, "Hey."

I turned my head, and there was Trina.

"What . . . ?" I must have blinked a thousand times, but the image before my eyes never changed. It was still Trina.

Only she wasn't at Luers.

And she wasn't not speaking to me.

"What are you *doing* here?" I finally managed to choke. "Did you miss the bus?"

"No," Trina said, taking out her own trig homework. "I quit, too."

"You quit. . . ." I could only gape at her. "Wait a minute. You quit *Troubadours*?"

Trina looked at me pityingly, like I was a little bit slow.

"Yeah," she said. "I quit Troubadours. What'd you get for number seven, anyway?"

"Wait a minute." I was having some real problems wrapping my mind around this one. I mean, Trina, the one person who I thought I'd be able to count on to back me up against Mr. Hall, hadn't done so. She hadn't uttered a word that day I'd thrown her hat into Jake Mancini's tuba.

And she hadn't said anything yesterday, either, when the sopranos had tried to rough me up in the caf.

But now she was sitting next to me at a time when surely she was supposed to be onstage at Bishop Luers, singing about slicking her hair and wearing her buckle shoes?

"You QUIT Troubadours?" I demanded, loudly enough that the librarian—who still hadn't thought to ask me why I was in the school library every day during fourth period and not in class—looked up from the checkout desk. So I lowered my voice. "Trina, what about your solo?"

"Karen Sue can do it," Trina said, turning back to her trig homework with a shrug.

"But . . ." I couldn't believe what I was hearing. "You love Troubadours, Trina."

"Not anymore," Trina said. Then, seeing my expression, she laid down her pencil and went, "Okay. Look. I'm sorry. I'm sorry I acted like such a spaz that day on your front porch. And I'm sorry I didn't come to your defense about the hat thing. Mr. Hall—he never should have said the things he said to you. I should have walked out with you, but . . . well, I was still too mad at you. But the more I thought about it, the madder I got . . . at *myself*, not you. I mean, it was my fault, not yours, that that hat went into the tuba. And that's not all." Trina took a deep breath. "You were right about Steve, too."

I blinked at her. "I was?" Now I *really* couldn't believe what I was hearing. *"Really?"*

"Yeah," Trina said. "He's a great guy, but I just never realized it until he . . . well, until he dumped me. Can you believe it?" She let out a little laugh. *"He* dumped *me*. And I *miss* him! Almost as much," she added, "as I miss you. You're a way better friend to me than I've ever been to you, Jen. I mean, I'm the one who made you sign up for choir in the first place. I should have warned you about the dancing. Or at least coached you more. Something."

"That's okay, Trina," I said, still playing it cool. Inside, though, I was doing cartwheels. I had my best friend back. I had my best friend back! "No amount of coaching would have helped."

"Well, probably not," Trina admitted. "But I still should have offered. I was just . . . jealous. You know? Over the Luke Striker thing. I *know* you guys are just friends. Believe me, I've heard you say it on the news enough times. But I couldn't help wondering . . . why didn't he want to be friends with *me*?"

I shrugged. I didn't feel like I could tell her the truth . . . that Luke hadn't wanted to be friends with her because he'd known she had a huge crush on him. And that he'd wanted to be friends with me because . . . well, I was starting to think it was because he thought of me as an interesting social experiment, and he was the mad scientist conducting it.

Instead I said, "I don't know. Guys are just weird, I guess."

"That's not it," Trina said, shaking her head. "I mean, that's not *just* it. The fact is, you're, like, a good person."

"Trina," I said, shaking my head with a laugh. "I'm so not. Were you *there* when I talked back to Mr. Hall? Have you *seen* what I've been up to lately?"

"Yes," Trina said. "And it's all good stuff. I mean, I was going to dump my boyfriend just so I could have a shot at going out with a movie star. How heinous was *that*? You not only kept that movie star's identity a secret—when you know anyone else would have been running around going, 'Luke Striker! Luke Striker!'—but you tried to keep the rest of us from, you know, objectifying him when we finally figured it out. And that thing you did with Cara—I mean, I'm not saying I like her or anything. Cara, I mean. But you took the time to show her how not to be such a wannabe. And now way less people want to kill her."

"Well," I said, not sure this was a compliment. "I guess. . . ."

"And now Betty Ann?" Trina shook her head at me. "Don't try to deny it. It's all over school. You just walked into Kurt's house and *took* her?"

"Well," I said, wondering how I was going to bring up the subject of Scott. Or if I even wanted to. It was all still so new, what I was feeling about him. . . . Besides, I knew exactly what Trina was going to say about it, if I told her. "Not exactly—"

"So really, how could I go with those guys to Luers?" Trina said, shrugging. "I mean, after you left, things just went from bad to worse. Hall was trying to get us all to call you and talk you into coming back. But not because—no offense, Jen—you're such a good singer or anything, but because he realized he'd lost his one claim to fame . . . the fact that Luke Striker's girlfriend was in his choir. Yes, I *know* you're just friends, but whatever. I was just like, *This is bogus.* So I didn't get on the bus this morning. It's like Ask Annie says."

I was a little surprised at hearing my secret pen name invoked in such a manner. "Like Ask Annie says? About what?"

"You know. Life's short. If you don't try new things, you'll never know what you're best at. And you can only make time for new things by quitting the things you *know* don't work for you."

"Huh," I said, like I'd never heard that one. "I guess that's true."

"What do you mean, you *guess* that's true?" Trina picked up her pencil. "Of course it's true. Annie said it. Do you even *read* her column? You know, it might do you some good."

It felt good, having my best friend back. I guess, in that way, Mrs. Mulvaney and I had a little something in common.

Except, of course, *my* best friend can actually speak.

It wasn't until the bell rang and Trina and I picked up our books and started to head down to the cafeteria that the librarian stopped us.

"Pardon me, Jenny," she said with an apologetic smile. She knew me because I check out books so often. I'd read every single thing she had on the sci-fi shelf. "I have to ask . . . do you or your friend here have passes? Because otherwise, I'm afraid I will have to report you for skipping class. I don't have either of you down for study hall this period. . . ."

There it was. Busted.

"Go ahead and mark us down," Trina said excitedly. Really. She was *excited* about being caught skipping class. "Catrina Larssen, with two *S*'s. And you know Jen, of course. We've quit Troubadours. You know, the show choir? I suppose they'll try to make us go back. But if they do, I'll have my mother call the school board, because Mr. Hall is trying to crush this poor girl's spirit." Trina threw an arm around me. "That's not right, is it? For a teacher to become abusive to a student, just because she can't get her jazz hands right? I mean, Jen can't help it if she's dance challenged. Her talents lie in other arenas."

The librarian stared at us with her mouth a little open. Then she said, "I see. Why don't you two, um, go on down to lunch right now, and I guess we'll . . . we'll just deal with this on Monday."

"Thanks," Trina said, with her biggest stage smile, the one you could see all the way to the last row of the auditorium. "See you then."

I was so, so glad Trina and I were friends again.

Especially when, later that day, it wasn't just Scott and me making the long walk across the parking lot to his car after school. We had Trina there, as well, since Scott had said, "Sure," when I'd asked him if it was okay if she hitched a ride with us after her play rehearsal, since she and Steve were broken up—and he, in any case, was away at Bishop Luers.

Trina hadn't looked a bit surprised when I'd told her Scott had been driving me home from school all week. She seemed to take it for granted that he would and that it was no big deal.

What I don't think Trina quite realized was that it *was* a

big deal. It was a *very* big deal. Because Scott and Geri were broken up. So it was just me and Scott in the car. *Alone.*

But I guess Trina just thought Scott and I were friends. Which we were. So being alone together in his car was perfectly fine. Which it was.

So why was I feeling so relieved that Trina was tagging along with us? Relieved and yet . . . well, a little bit disappointed?

Whatever. I'd given up trying to analyze my feelings. There were just too *many* of them lately, for some reason.

We were strolling toward Scott's car, just the three of us, talking about how we couldn't wait for summer vacation and what we were going to do during it—Trina, theater camp; Scott, internship at the local paper; me, baby-sitting (of course)—when something totally unexpected happened. This giant bus pulled into the parking lot. Not a school bus or a Greyhound bus or anything, but, like, a tour bus. It pulled up to the back of the school, and the motor stopped.

Trina, arrested by this sight, froze in her tracks.

"Oh my God," she said, staring at the bus. "Why are they back so early? They shouldn't be back so early. Not unless . . ."

We heard the sound of the bus door opening. Then, a second later, I recognized Mr. Hall's voice, shouting at everyone not to leave until they were sure they had all their things from the bus.

". . . they didn't make the finals," Trina said.

And sure enough, one of the first people to come out from behind the bus, the garment bag containing his tuxedo thrown over one shoulder, was Trina's ex-boyfriend Steve. He didn't notice her right away, standing there staring at him, because he was digging in the pocket of his jeans for his car keys.

Then, as Scott and I stood there watching, Trina did the most surprising thing. You know, considering she and Steve were broken up and all, and she'd just been telling me how murderously angry with him she was for dumping her the way he had, just a few days before the most important dance of the school year. Except, of course, that because of his dumping her, she'd realized Steve was her soul mate and that she would never love anyone as much as she loved him. Not even Luke Striker.

What Trina did was say his name.

That's all. Just his name.

But it carried, you know. Across the parking lot. Because she'd been practicing her projection so much, at night in her bedroom.

Steve looked up and seemed to go immobile with shock. Trina was clearly the last person he'd been expecting to see.

He wasn't too happy about seeing her, either.

"Oh, *great*," he said, when he saw her. Steve's projection

isn't too shabby, either. Well, it has to be good, you know, for him to play her leading men. The Clayton High School Drama Club can't afford a sound system with microphones and stuff. "*There* you are."

"Steve," Trina said again. But Steve wouldn't let her go on.

"Oh, no," he said, holding up a hand—the one with the car keys in it—to stop her when she took a step toward him. "No, you don't. Do you have any idea what I've been through for the past ten hours? I had to get on that bus at six in the morning. Six A.M., Trina. With a bunch of sopranos singing 'Ninety-nine Bottles of Beer on the Wall.' In two-part harmony. At *dawn.*"

Scott and I watched, fascinated, as Steve stabbed an index finger in Trina's direction. I had to admit, this was good. I had never seen Steve's Adam's apple bob so much.

"And *why*?" Steve demanded, seemingly of no one in particular. Or maybe of all of us. "Because my *ex-girlfriend* begged me to. Begged me to join her stupid freaking choir. So I did. And then I find out—too late, of course, because I'm already *on* the freaking bus—that my *ex-girlfriend* didn't even bother to show up. So then I have to sit on that bus for *three hours* before going onstage and standing there in a rented tux, like a total jerk, singing about my *buckle shoes* in front of freaking *Miss Kentucky.* Who thought we sucked, by the way. Well, you know what, Trina? *I quit.*"

And to emphasize his point, Steve threw the garment bag containing his tuxedo onto the asphalt. Then stomped on it.

"I *quit,*" he yelled. A lot of the other Troubadours had come out from behind the bus and, hearing all the commotion, were standing there staring at Steve and Trina, just like we were. I saw Kwang with his Palm Pilot and Jake Mancini with his tuba and Karen Sue Walters, looking sort of stunned by the whole thing, with her red sequined dress dangling limply from its hanger.

Mr. Hall was there, too, an expression of undisguised horror on his face as he watched his best baritone mangle his Deluxe Tux rental.

"I *quit,*" Steve yelled. "No more plays. No more musicals. And no more show choir, Trina. It's over. I'm sick of signing up for this stuff just to make you happy. I'm going to do what I wanted to do in the first place." He stopped stomping on the tux and glared at her, his chest heaving up and down. "Next year, I'm joining the baseball team."

Every head in the parking lot swiveled toward Trina to see what her reaction would be. Including mine.

Trina's performance did not disappoint. She hadn't been Steve's leading lady in all those plays for nothing. She tossed her long, silky hair back, then held out her arms.

Then she said, "Anything you want, baby. I love you."

And Steve, with a muffled cry that appeared to be filled with as much frustration as it was adoration, snatched her up and covered her mouth with his . . .

. . . to the satisfaction of everyone in their audience . . . with the possible exception of Mr. Hall, who turned around and stormed off to his Jetta without another word to anyone.

It was pretty obvious after that that Trina wasn't going to ride home with Scott and me. Which was just as well. I was a little stunned by the display of unbridled passion I'd just witnessed. I hadn't seen kissing like that since . . . well, never.

I suppose it hadn't been as shocking to Scott. You know, given all the hearts in Geri Lynn's date book. Because he still seemed capable of human speech.

"So, Jen," he said, as we turned on to my street. "About you and Luke . . ."

"We're just friends." That, at least, I could say. I mean, I'd had enough practice at it.

"Yeah," Scott said. "I know that. I mean, I know that's what you tell the media. But, I mean. This is me."

"We're just friends," I said again. But I said it differently this time. Because I'd turned my head to look at him. And I could tell this hadn't been just a casual question. Scott really wanted to know.

"I *know*," Scott said. He looked . . . I don't know. For a second, I thought he looked kind of . . . angry.

Only why should Scott be angry at me? What did *I* do?

"But . . . it's true," I said, not knowing what else to say.

"Yeah," Scott said, in a different voice. "I know."

And at that moment, we pulled up in front of my house. And the usual flock of news reporters descended upon Scott's car, all pointing microphones toward the passenger side window . . . my window.

*"Miss Greenley? Miss Greenley, is it true that you're going to co-star with Luke Striker in his next film?"*

"Scott," I said, again, worriedly. What was *wrong* with him?

But maybe I'd just imagined the whole mad-at-me thing. Because a second later, Scott smiled at me and said, "You better make a run for it while there's still only thirty or forty of them out there."

I laughed at his joke. A little weakly.

"Okay," I said. "Um. See you."

"Right," he said. "See you Monday."

See you Monday. Right. Because I was going to the Spring Fling tomorrow night with Luke. And Scott wasn't going at all. So I wouldn't be seeing him again until Monday. Why did this realization make me feel like someone had stuck a hand in my chest and ripped out my heart?

I was still feeling that way when the phone rang later that night, and it was Trina, gushing about how she was going to the Spring Fling after all, and that I should see her dress—she'd finally managed to talk her mother into letting her wear black.

"Huh," was all I could think of to say.

Trina didn't appear to notice my lack of talkativeness.

"So what's up with Scott, anyway?" Trina wanted to know.

My chest suddenly felt tight. She'd noticed. Trina had noticed. That I think I might like Scott. Oh, no. She'd noticed.

"What do you mean?" I asked anxiously.

"Well, who's this girl Geri says he likes?"

My heart did a somersault in my chest, proving it hadn't been ripped out after all. "Girl? What girl?"

"You know. This mystery girl Geri thinks Scott likes. Well, you've heard her going on about it."

It was true, I had heard Geri. But I had been trying very hard to tune her out. Because I don't want to hear about Scott liking some other girl.

Some girl other than me.

"God," Trina said. "Wouldn't it be funny if it turned out the girl Scott's in love with is *you*?"

"Yeah," I said, squeezing the phone so tightly I was surprised it didn't shoot out of my hand and go flying across the room.

"No, I'm serious," Trina said. "I mean, he's been giving you rides every day. And you guys like the same books—you know, those end-of-the-world books. Wouldn't it be wild if the girl it turns out Scott's secretly in love with is you?"

"Scott's not in love with me," I said sadly. *See you Monday.* Yeah, not what a guy says when he's in love with you.

"Yeah, you're probably right," Trina said dismissively. "Besides, you've got Luke."

"Luke and I are just—"

"Oh my God, I get the picture," Trina said.

Except that she didn't. No one did.

Least of all, I was starting to think, me.

# Ask Annie

Ask Annie your most complex interpersonal relationship questions. Go on, we dare you! All letters to Annie are subject to publication in the Clayton High School *Register*. Names and e-mail addresses of correspondents guaranteed confidential.

Dear Annie,

I read your column every week, and I think you give terrible advice. You told that girl whose stepmother was only looking out for her immortal soul not to worry about hell . . . that she was already in it.

Annie, high school is not hell. High school is supposed to be some of the best years of a person's life. And for anyone who attends church regularly and stays away from sex, drugs, alcohol, and rock music, they can be.

It's just people like you, Annie, who ruin high school for everyone by espousing free love and Satanism.

Outraged Teen

Dear Outraged,

How do you know I worship Satan? You

don't know anything about me.

And I happen to agree with you about the drugs and alcohol, and—with the exception of safe sex—the sex thing, too.

But rock music? No way, dude. Rock rules, and always will.

Annie

## Sixteen

*They say the* second most important day of a woman's life, after her wedding day, is her junior-senior formal.

Well, okay, probably the birth of her first child is up there somewhere, too.

But you get what I mean.

I spent mine—the day of my junior-senior formal—doing all the prom-y things every girl does. You know, the manicure and pedicure, the waxing (*ouch*), the blow out at the hair salon.

Of course, I was the only girl in America who, while getting ready for her prom, had a phalanx of reporters following her around, trying to get photos of the girl who was going to the prom with America's sweetheart getting her upper lip bleached. Thanks for that, guys. No, really.

It was kind of annoying, but, hey, I'd promised a friend I'd go to the Spring Fling with him. I owed it to him to look my best.

And when I'd slipped into my dress—a blue satiny number, covered with a layer of chiffon, with little poofy chiffony sleeves and little chiffony forget-me-nots all around the hem . . . the girliest dress you ever saw—I felt like I actually *looked* my best. The hairstylist had clipped back my not-fully-grown-out-yet bangs with a barrette that even had real live blue forget-me-nots on it, just like the fake ones around my feet.

Trina had called me and arranged for the two of us to meet in my front yard so that we could pose for photos together for our parents. The fact that every entertainment program from *Access Hollywood* to *Rank* had a van parked outside my house to capture the moment Luke pulled up in his limo didn't seem to faze Trina a bit.

We met, as planned, by the huge oak tree in my front yard, and commenced to admire each other, even as all around us cameras—and not just the ones belonging to our parents—whirred.

Trina had been able to convince her mother to let her go Village Goth for the Spring Fling. She'd forgone the black lipstick, but she'd still managed to hunt up black fishnets, which she wore with black Converse high-tops. Her dress consisted of a gauzy black thing straight out of the pages of the *Seventeen* prom issue . . .

. . . but she'd fastened a black silk bustier over it, so her not-unremarkable bosom swelled to impressive heights over the neckline.

I couldn't tell who was more likely to have a heart attack when he saw her, Steve or Dr. Lewis.

"I cannot believe," I said, "that you talked your mother into letting you wear that."

"I cannot believe," Trina said, "that you let your mother talk *you* into wearing *that*."

"Hideously traditional," I said. "I know."

"Still," Trina said. "You look nice."

"So do you." Because she did. I was gladder than ever that we were friends again.

We heard the limo coming long before we saw it, because photographers who'd climbed trees around our street, hoping to get an unimpeded shot of Luke pinning on my corsage, started shouting excitedly to one another, "Here he comes! Here he comes!"

Even I—who could not seem really to work up the kind of enthusiasm that, say, Trina had for the occasion—felt a little thrill of excitement. Oh, well. I wasn't going to the Spring Fling with someone I loved, it was true.

But at least I was going to the Spring Fling.

Then the limo came into sight, the same long black sleek one that I'd taken to Luke's condo at the lake and back. Trina squeezed my hand excitedly as the vehicle came to a slow stop in front of my house, and the driver got out and went around to open the passenger side door.

Every photographer—every cameraperson, every parent—in the vicinity lifted their camera to snap a shot of Luke Striker emerging from his limo, like Lancelot on his white horse when he swooped down to rescue Guenevere from being burned to death at the stake.

But the person who emerged from the limo wasn't Luke Striker. The person who came out, carrying a corsage and waving to all the camerapeople, was none other than . . .

Steve McKnight.

That's right. Steve McKnight, Trina's boyfriend and Spring Fling date, in his Troubadours tux (though he'd traded in his red bow tie and cummerbund for black ones).

The reporters sighed—some of them even booed—and went back to their stakeout.

Trina, however, was absolutely delighted.

"I can't believe you rented a limo," she squealed, as Steve pinned on her corsage—a bunch of carnations that he had, as Trina had instructed him to, let sit overnight in a bottle of black ink, so that the white petals were now tinged with black. "It must have cost you a fortune!"

"Uh," Steve said, looking kind of embarrassed. "Not really."

"Oh, your parents paid for it?" Trina asked, as the two of

them posed for photos in front of Trina's excited mom and dad.

"Uh," Steve said. "Actually, Luke Striker did."

Trina froze.

She wasn't the only one, either.

"*Luke* did?" Trina glanced at me worriedly. "What . . . why?"

"I don't know," Steve said with an awkward shrug. "He said he didn't need it anymore."

"Didn't . . ." Trina's gaze on me grew pitying. She realized what was happening before I did. Or thought she did, anyway. "Oh, Jen. Look, it doesn't matter. It doesn't. You can come with us. We'll have a ball. Won't we, Steve?"

"Sure," Steve said. "Of course."

I still didn't get it. So Luke had given Steve his limo? Big deal. That didn't mean Luke wasn't coming.

Luke wouldn't stand me up. Not in front of all these reporters. After all, what had I ever done to deserve treatment like that? Just been his friend. Kept his secret.

CHANGED CLAYTON HIGH FROM A PLACE FILLED WITH ANGST AND ANTAGONISM INTO THE WARM AND ACCEPTING SCHOOL IT WAS TODAY FOR HIM.

"Oh, honey," my mom said, coming over to give me a hug. The photographers, starting to realize what had happened, lifted their cameras to get a shot of that. I could just see the headlines the next day.

## AMERICA'S SWEETHEART JILTS JEN!
## A MOTHER'S LOVE ONLY BALM FOR
## BROKENHEARTED JENNY!
## THAT DIRTY RAT!

But before my mom had a chance to say any of the words of comfort she'd thought up, a cry rose from the treetops.

And the next thing I knew, a guy in a tux had pulled up in front of Steve's limousine . . . on a motorcycle.

A Harley, no less.

"Hey," Luke said, as he pulled off his black helmet. "Sorry I'm late."

The yard was ablaze with flashes. Reporters were screaming, "Luke! Luke! Look this way, Luke!"

Luke completely ignored them. He walked straight up to my dad and stuck his right hand out.

"Mr. Greenley, sir," he said. "I'm Luke Striker. I'm here to take your daughter to the Spring Fling."

My dad, for possibly the first time in his life, looked as if he didn't know quite what to do. Finally, he took Luke's hand in his and shook it.

"How do you do," he said.

Then he seemed to recover himself. He said, "You expect to take Jenny to the formal on *that*?"

"No," my mother said, shaking her head. "Absolutely not without a helmet."

"There's an extra helmet under the seat, Mrs. Greenley," Luke said, taking her hand and giving it a shake as well. "And I swear I'll have her home by midnight."

I elbowed him.

"I mean one," Luke said.

"I'll call you if I'm going to be later than that," I said, and grabbed Luke by the arm. "Bye."

"Wait!" my mother called. "We didn't get a picture!"

But my mom didn't have to worry. Because every periodical in America—with the exception maybe of *National Geographic*, who didn't seem to have sent a representative—got a picture of Luke helping me put the spare helmet on over my flowered hair clip. Of Luke helping me onto the back of the bike without getting any grease on my skirt, and of Luke wrapping that skirt around my legs so it wouldn't catch in the wheel spokes and strangle and or drag me to my death. Of Luke waving as he stepped on the accelerator. Of me grabbing Luke around the waist and holding on for dear life.

And of the two of us zooming down the street as fast as we could go without breaking the speed limit or worse, upsetting my parents.

"I hope you don't mind," Luke said later, after we'd pulled up in front of the Clayton Inn—where we were met by more reporters . . . the ones who'd been able to beat us from my house, of which there weren't many. "About the bike, I mean."

"It's fine," I said. I had actually really enjoyed it. I'd never been on a motorcycle before. Nice girls like me don't generally get asked to ride them. "But I thought you wanted a typical prom experience. And arriving at the prom on a Harley? Hate to break it to you, Luke, but that's not so typical."

"Well," Luke said, reaching up to fix one of the flowers on my hair clip. "I always like to make a big entrance. Oh, I almost forgot."

And from beneath the motorcycle's seat, he withdrew a clear plastic box, inside of which lay a corsage made of white roses and baby's breath.

"Oh, it's beautiful," I said. Then I remembered the boutonniere I'd left in the fridge back home. "I forgot yours at the house!"

"We are *not* going back there," Luke declared, expertly pinning the corsage into place, just above my heart. "I'll survive without one."

Then he offered me his arm. "Madam. Shall we dance?"

"So long as we don't have to use jazz hands," I said.

"Have no fear. I called ahead to check. This event is guaranteed jazz hands free."

With this assurance, I took Luke's arm, and the two of us glided into the Clayton Inn—flashes going off all around us, and reporters—not to mention actual residents of Clayton, who'd crowded the inn's driveway for a chance to see their favorite star and his date for the evening—screaming our names.

I don't want you to get the wrong impression. Like that the Spring Fling is fun or anything. I mean, even if you go with the most popular teenage movie star in America—maybe even the world—the Spring Fling is still kind of a drag.

It's true that you get to see everyone from school looking better than you've ever seen them.

But, you know, they're still the people that you see every day at school. Just shinier. And maybe, you know, cleaner.

I didn't have it half so bad as *some* girls. There were *some* girls there who you just knew were destined for a bad time. Like Karen Sue Walters, for instance. She had shanghaied one of the tenors into going with her. One of the tenors who everyone in the whole school knew was completely gaga for Luke Striker. The whole time they were dancing, Karen Sue's date kept gazing longingly in the direction of Luke's tuxedo pants.

It was actually kind of amusing.

Which was really the best part of Spring Fling. You know, the part where we all made fun of it. It turned out Luke was really good at it. We all sat at the same table—me; Luke;

Trina; Steve; Bored Liz and her date (one of the football players. Don't ask); and Tough Brenda and her date, a surprisingly nice, soft-spoken guy named Lamar—and made fun of the food and the music and, finally, everyone there.

The dancing didn't start until the food had been cleared away. Then everyone drifted out onto the dance floor . . . including me and Luke. I told Luke I could only handle the slow ones—I was still suffering from post-traumatic stress syndrome from my whole Troubadour experience—and he said he understood.

Luke, it turned out, was a terrific dancer . . . big surprise, right? He was so good that he almost made up for me sucking so badly at it. Our knees only collided like half a dozen times, and I think I only kicked him once.

I don't know what Luke was thinking about as he held me close during our slow dances together. I can only tell you what I was thinking about.

Or who, actually.

And that was . . . well, not Luke.

I know! It really was awful. I have to be the most ungrateful girl in the history of time. I mean, there I was, with this great—*really* great—Spring Fling date, this guy who had worked hard to make the Spring Fling as fun for me as the Spring Fling could be—or, at least, as fun as a Spring Fling you were attending with someone in whom you weren't romantically interested could be—and I couldn't stop thinking about someone else!

It was pathetic, is what it was.

But not as pathetic as my reaction a minute later when I spotted, just past Luke's shoulder, a familiar figure in a slinky, low-cut gown of pale peach.

Geri Lynn! What was Geri Lynn doing at the Spring Fling? Could she have found a date so soon after breaking up with Scott?

No way. Or I would have heard about it.

Which could only mean one thing.

I lifted my head from Luke's chest and started looking around. He had to be here somewhere. I mean, if Geri was here . . .

I felt Luke chuckle, deep in his chest.

"Relax, Jen," he said. "She came alone."

I pretended not to know what he was talking about. What else could I do?

"Who?" I asked.

"You know who I'm talking about," Luke said. In the "romantic" lighting—really just purple gels slipped over the reception room's normal lights and one of those big glittery disco balls . . . which Luke swore he hadn't seen anywhere since his character's prom on *Heaven Help Us*—his face still looked incredibly attractive.

And though I couldn't, in the half-light, tell that his eyes were blue, I could tell that his gaze was on mine, with somewhat disconcerting directness.

"I'm onto you, Jen Greenley," he said.

I squinted at him. "I beg your pardon?"

"I'm onto you," he said again. "Not just about that, either. I've got you completely worked out. You're Annie, aren't you?"

I nearly choked. "Wh-what?"

"You're Ask Annie," Luke said, "from the school newspaper."

I blinked. I couldn't believe he even knew what Ask Annie was.

And that he was bringing it up *now*. At the *Spring Fling*.

"Are you kidding?" he said, when I mentioned this. "Everybody talks about her. Ask Annie says this. Ask Annie says that. You're, like, the unofficial school psychologist."

I have to admit that hearing this gave me a nice tingling feeling. I would totally have *loved* to be the school psychologist. If I were, the first thing I'd do is abolish mandatory attendance at pep rallies. I mean, how are you supposed to feel peppy about crushing your opponent? It was just so wrong. Wasn't your opponent going to feel bad for losing? That's the only reason I never went to the games. I could barely look at the faces of the team who lost. It was just so *sad*.

The second thing I'd abolish? The Spring Fling.

"I don't get why it's a big secret, though," Luke said.

I gave up the pretense. He knew. I was just going to have to deal.

"Oh." I shrugged. "That's easy. Because if people knew who Ask Annie was, they wouldn't necessarily trust her to be neutral."

"And you think that's what you are?" Luke asked. "Neutral?"

Was he kidding? Did he not know that I was—or used to be, anyway—the most neutral person on the planet?

He had to be kidding.

He wasn't kidding.

"Because I haven't noticed you acting too neutral lately," he went on. "I mean, that thing with Cara—"

"She needed my help," I interrupted. I mean, this should have been obvious to him.

"And the Troubadours thing?"

"Troubadours wasn't for me," I said. Duh.

"And Betty Ann? When you ruined the senior prank? How neutral was that?"

"Oh, well, that—"

And then I dropped my arms from around his neck and took a step backward so I could look at him . . . *really* look at him.

"Hey," I said. "How'd you know about Betty Ann?" I narrowed my eyes at him. "Did Steve tell you?"

"Not Steve," Luke said. "But, like I said, I have my sources."

Around us, the music had stopped. Dr. Lewis and Juicy Lucy, who were—unfortunately—our chaperones for the evening, mounted the dais at the end of the room. Dr. Lewis tapped on the microphone in front of the dais.

"Testing," he said, and blew on it. "Testing. One. Two. Three."

"Let me ask you a question," Luke said, reaching out to take my hand. "And I don't want neutrality. I want Ask Annie, who is about as neutral as nitroglycerin. I really want to know what you think about this."

"Um, hello, everyone, and welcome to Clayton High School's annual Spring Fling," Dr. Lewis read into the microphone from an index card.

"Shoot," I said to Luke.

"Okay," Luke said. "Let's say there was this guy. And he happened to be in love with this girl—"

"I don't want to keep you all from the party," Dr. Lewis said. "So let's get right down to it. The votes have been tallied for this year's Spring Fling king and queen."

"—and let's say that for some reason—never mind what that reason is—the girl decided to break up with him," Luke went on. "How long do you think he'd have to wait before he could move on to . . . someone else? And not, you know, risk being accused of being on the rebound?"

"I don't know," I said. What was Luke talking about? *Who* was Luke talking about? Who had been dumped by a girl lately? No one I knew.

Then suddenly, my hands—including the one Luke was holding—began to sweat. Geri Lynn, I saw, had noticed us. She waved gaily. Scott was most definitely *not* with her. He might have been somewhere else in the room . . . but he wasn't with Geri.

Was *that* who Luke was talking about? Scott, I mean? Scott had recently been dumped. . . .

That had to be who he was talking about. Scott. Scott Bennett. Scott had asked Luke to ask me how long he'd have to wait before he could ask out the mystery girl, the one he liked. . . . Of course he had! He certainly couldn't ask Annie. Not without my knowing it was him. So he'd had Luke do it for him.

"As you know," Dr. Lewis droned into the microphone, "there was a table set up in the cafeteria all week, where you could write in your votes for Spring Fling king and queen. Well, those votes have been tallied, and I'm happy to say, we have our winners!"

"Not winners," Juicy Lucy interrupted hastily. "Everyone

here is a winner. Dr. Lewis meant to say we have our Spring Fling king and queen."

"Yes," Dr. Lewis said. "Yes, that's what I meant. And the king and queen of the Clayton High School Spring Fling are . . . Oh, dear. Well, this is a bit unusual. One of the, er, members of the royal party isn't exactly . . . I mean, doesn't exactly go to Clayton High. . . ."

"I think," I said to Luke, even as Geri Lynn was making a beeline for us. "I think he should wait. I think he should wait a really, *really* long time. Because, you know, he wouldn't want to rush into anything. The right girl might be right around the corner, you know. Maybe even closer than he thinks. And he should wait until he's *totally sure* he's found her. . . ."

"That's what I was hoping you'd say," Luke said.

And then he dropped my hand, turned around, and scooped Geri Lynn up in his arms.

"Hi ya, babe," he said to her.

And kissed her.

On the lips.

And didn't stop kissing her, even after Dr. Lewis said into the microphone, "Oh, what the hay. I'd be proud to call him an honorary Clayton Rooster. This year's Clayton High Spring Fling king and queen are . . . *Luke Striker and Jenny Greenley!*"

# Ask Annie

Ask Annie your most complex interpersonal relationship
questions. Go on, we dare you! All letters to Annie are subject
to publication in the Clayton High School *Register*. Names and
e-mail addresses of correspondents guaranteed confidential.

Dear Annie,
I love him. He doesn't know I'm alive. What
do I do now?
     Desperate

Dear Desperate,
When you figure it out, could you please let
me know?
     Because I haven't got the foggiest idea.

                    Annie

# Seventeen

*"It's just,"* *Luke* said, as we shared our spotlight dance—a requisite part, it turned out, of our coronation ceremony—"I was so sure after Angelique left me that I'd never love again. And then I met Geri Lynn, and . . . I don't know. It wasn't love at first sight or anything. I swear it. It happened gradually."

Right. Gradually, over a period of less than two weeks—most of which he'd spent in Los Angeles.

"I know we're completely different," he went on—probably the first Spring Fling king in the history of Clayton High to spend his entire dance with the queen talking instead of making out, like a normal guy—"I mean, she wants to be a *reporter*. And you know how I hate the stalkarazzi. But some of the things she said in that essay—you know, the pro-con one Scott had us write?—got me thinking. She's not like other girls, you know. She's not afraid to speak her mind."

Wasn't *that* the truth.

"There may be some truth to the fact that we celebrities need the media. And of course they need us. It's a symbiotic relationship I'd never given much thought to before. But Geri *made* me think about it," Luke explained. "That's what I like so much about her. She makes me think, you know? When she gave me her number, that day at the car wash, I wasn't going to call her. But then . . . I don't know. I thought I'd been a little rough on you that day at the condo. You know, about the whole special sauce thing. So I phoned Geri and asked her to look out for you . . . just to give me a call if she thought you were getting in over your head with the reporters or whatever. I figured if anyone would know whether they were being too rough with you, it was her. I started calling her a couple times a day, just to touch base about you . . . and pretty soon, you know, we went from talking about you . . . to talking about her . . . to talking about me and her. . . .Well, you know how it goes."

Oh, I *definitely* know how it goes. Geri Lynn is a total expert at snagging boys out from under my nose.

No. That wasn't fair. I'd never wanted Luke.

And I was happy for him. I really was. For him and for Geri Lynn. They made a nice couple. He was totally gorgeous, and so was Geri. He was only a year older than she was, after all. And she was heading off for college in L.A., where Luke happened to live.

True, Geri was going to major in journalism, and Luke didn't happen to be all that fond of journalists. But Geri didn't seem all that fond of "theater types." So maybe they were even.

Whatever. What did they need *my* blessing for?

"It's just that you're so incredible," Luke droned on, the fake jewels in his oversize Spring Fling king crown winking in the spotlight. "Really, really incredible, Jen. What you did, in just a week, at that school . . . it's unbelievable. Geri thinks you should run for student body president next year. I couldn't agree more."

"I don't know," I said. "I'm not all that interested in politics."

"Well, get interested," Luke said. "Because you're a natural. At least promise me you'll think about it."

"Yeah," I said, mostly to get him off my back. "Okay, I'll think about it. Listen. About the Ask Annie thing. Did you really just figure that one out? Or did Geri find out somehow—" Um, because Scott, her boyfriend, told her, for instance? "—and tell you?"

"Figured it out myself," Luke said. "And don't worry. I won't tell her. Just like I'm not going to tell her about the other thing."

"What other thing?" I asked him, not for one iota of a

second expecting him to say what he did next, which was:

"You know. That you're in love with her ex."

It was a good thing our spotlight dance ended just then, or everyone at the Clayton High School Spring Fling might have gotten a real good look at my tonsils. Because I'm pretty sure that's how wide my mouth fell open at the words *in love with her ex.*

"I am not," I stood there and blathered like an idiot. "I most certainly am not . . . in love . . . with . . . Scott Bennett."

"Why don't you take your own advice, Jen?" Luke asked me, as we were joined on the dance floor by dozens of other couples. "Why don't you let him know how you feel?"

"Th-that was my advice for *you*," I stammered. "I mean, for Scott. I mean . . . Oh, I don't know *what* I mean."

"Well," Luke said, as Geri Lynn suddenly appeared, beaming, at his side. "I don't know what you mean, either. But I do know one thing."

"What's that?" I asked him.

"There's a limo waiting outside that will take you any-where you want to go."

"Huh," I said, because that information was of absolutely no use to me whatsoever. "Thanks."

And then he drifted off to sign a few autographs for some people who simply couldn't help themselves and came up with their Spring Fling programs, begging.

"Look, are you really okay about this?" Geri asked me, as soon as he was gone. "I mean, about Luke and me?"

"Oh God, yes," I said, meaning it. "I told you, we're just friends."

"You're the best, Jen," Geri said, giving my hand a squeeze. "None of this would have happened without you. I'm just so happy! I can't thank you enough. Like Luke said, you really are special."

Yeah. I was special all right. That's why my date for the Spring Fling had walked out on me.

I told Geri I was happy for her (again) and drifted back to our table, where Steve was giving Trina a foot rub. Apparently it's possible to get blisters on Spring Fling night even if your new shoes happen to be sneakers.

"Geri Lynn is such a skank," were the cheerful words with which I was greeted by Trina. "Imagine her scamming on your man. And right in front of you!"

"Relax, Trina," I said. "I told them both it was all right. Luke and I are—"

"Just friends," echoed Trina, Steve, Bored Liz, Tough Brenda, and their dates.

"Well, we are," I said a little defensively. Why wouldn't anyone believe me?

"The Spring Fling sucks," Trina observed a second later. "You know what I wish? I wish we hadn't even come to this stupid thing. I wish we had gone to Kwang's anti–Spring Fling party instead. I bet those guys are having a lot more fun than we are."

And that was when it hit me.

What Luke had said about using the limo, I mean.

"Why don't we?" I said, my heart thumping a little uncomfortably beneath Luke's corsage. "Go to Kwang's party. It's early—only ten o'clock. The party's probably just getting started."

"I heard he was going to have a campfire," Bored Liz said, looking visibly less bored.

"I heard he was gonna have illegal fireworks," Tough Brenda said with relish.

"Let's go," I said. "Luke said we could take the limo."

Trina blinked. "Are you serious?"

"Sure," I said. "What does he need the limo for? He's got the Harley."

"Time," Steve said, putting down Trina's foot, "to motor."

We didn't bother saying good-bye to Luke and Geri. That's because they were too busy making out on the dance floor to be interrupted. I could see Dr. Lewis eyeing them uncertainly.

There wasn't much he could do about the situation, of course. Geri was eighteen, a legal adult. If she and Luke wanted to rent a room at the inn later—hey, who could stop them?

Still, I would lay money on Juicy Lucy trying to.

I thought a little dejectedly of tomorrow's headlines. You know, when the press found out I'd been ditched by Luke for another girl.

Or maybe they'd work it from the other angle. You know, the one where I'd ditched Luke at the Spring Fling to go to another party. You never know. It could happen.

When the limo driver pulled up in front of Kwang's place—which was this huge white farmhouse way out in the country with a big barn and cornfields and its own woods with a stream running through it and everything . . . the perfect place to have loud parties complete with campfires and illegal fireworks—he said kind of skeptically, "Is this really where you want to be?"

Our only response was an enthusiastic, "Yes, thanks!" as we tumbled out of the car and ran for the distant glow of the campfire.

Everybody was there. Well, everybody who hadn't been at the Spring Fling, anyway. There were long picnic tables piled high with chips and sodas, and a stereo system attached to two enormous speakers booming loudly enough to be heard by over half the county, practically.

Kwang was sitting in front of the roaring campfire with a

stick in his hand. At the end of the stick was a marshmallow. Seated beside Kwang was Cara Schlosburg. In her lap was an opened packet of graham crackers and some half-eaten chocolate bars. They giggled guiltily as we came up.

And if the thin strand of gooey marshmallow that ran from Kwang's mouth to Cara's was any indication, I knew that they weren't exactly feeling guilty over having gone off their diets.

But none of us chose to go there. At least not then. Instead, everyone gathered around, clamoring for their own sticks and marshmallows, yammering on about what happened at the Spring Fling. The story of me winning Spring Fling queen proved to be a crowd pleaser. I heard a familiar laugh and turned around . . .

. . . and there was Scott, sitting on a log on the other side of the campfire.

And I knew. Just like that.

Well, not *just* like that. I mean, my heart did some pretty serious turning over in my chest. And suddenly I felt like I couldn't breathe. Those were pretty strong indicators.

It's just that at that moment, I finally knew what they were indicators of:

That I was in love with Scott Bennett. That I had been in love with him my whole life, practically. Suddenly, all of these images flashed before my campfire-dazzled eyes—

Scott's name above mine on the checkout card for *The Andromeda Strain*; Scott getting out of his car in the parking lot, years later, that day we left for the retreat; Scott lifting me toward that log; Scott going over my ad copy layout; Scott chasing me around the Chi-Chi's parking lot with that bucket; Scott helping me rescue Betty Ann. . . .

And I knew. I finally knew. What Trina had known all along. Luke, too, apparently.

But until that moment, I'd had no idea.

But I did now.

Which is why I did what I did next. Which was walk over and plunk myself right down beside him, resolutely ignoring my staggering pulse, suddenly shallow breath, and, most of all, the nagging conviction that I might be too late. Again.

"Hi," I said to Scott. I don't even know how I got the word out, but I did.

"Hi," Scott said. "Is that the Hope diamond? Or an uncannily realistic replica?"

I went, "What?" Then, "Oh," as I reached up and was embarrassed to realize I was still wearing my crown. I took it off and set it on the log between us. "Sorry. I'm a queen."

"I always thought so," Scott said gallantly. "Marshmallow?"

He presented me with the one he'd been carefully roasting on the end of the stick he held.

"Sure," I said, and peeled it gingerly from the stick. "Thanks."

"So." Scott slid another marshmallow onto the stick and put it in the flames. "Spring Fling over?"

"Oh, no," I said. "It's still going on."

And suddenly I remembered who was still there. At the Spring Fling, I mean. Luke. And Geri. Scott's ex-girlfriend. What if he asked me? What if he asked what had happened to my date? Was it really true about him being in love with someone else? What if it was Geri he still cared about?

"Weren't you having a good time?" he asked.

"Oh, no," I said, more lightly than I actually felt. "I was."

"What happened to Luke?"

And there it was.

"Well," I began slowly.

But it turned out I didn't even have to go on. Because Scott went, "You know, don't you? About Geri?"

I hadn't eaten the marshmallow he'd given me. I don't think I could have eaten anything just then if I'd tried. So when he said that, well, my hands went sort of numb, and the marshmallow, even sticky as it was, slipped from my fingers and fell into a gloppy mess at my feet.

"*You* know?" My voice cracked.

Scott looked down at the marshmallow. "Yeah. Geri told me."

"When?"

"Yesterday."

*Yesterday?* "Why didn't you tell *me*?"

"I tried to," he said. "In the car, remember?"

*That* was what that had been about?

"I guess I should have tried harder. But—" Scott presented me with a new marshmallow, perfectly golden on the outside. "I thought . . . well, I thought you might get upset."

I dropped the second one, too.

"*Upset?* About Luke and Geri?" I stared at him. "Why would *that* make me upset?"

He looked surprised. "Well, because—"

"Oh my God," Trina said, collapsing onto the log next to me. "Did you get a load of that strand of marshmallow goo between Cara and Kwang? 'Fess up, Scott. Were those two making out before we got here?"

"I don't know," Scott said.

When I glanced over at Scott again, I found him looking at me, not Trina. I would venture to say he was looking at me intently, but the truth was, I could only judge that from the fact that his head wasn't moving. I couldn't see his eyes, because the flames from the campfire had cast them into deep shadow.

I swear, though, the way he was looking at me, for a minute, I almost thought . . .

Well, I almost thought maybe *I* was the mystery girl he was supposedly in love with. And that, you know, he hadn't said anything because—

"Well, *I* think they were making out," Trina went on, "and with their mouths full. I'm sorry, but if Steve ever tried to kiss me with his mouth full of s'mores, I'd be all, See ya, dude. Even if he is, you know, my soul mate and all."

"Jen," Scott said to me suddenly. "Do you want to go for a walk?"

Trina looked at him like he was crazy.

"Don't go for a walk *now*," she said. "The fireworks are about to start."

But if anybody thinks I was going to give up a walk with Scott for an illegal fireworks show . . . well, I'd have to say they're nuts.

"Sure," I said, somehow managing to sound casual, even though my heart was in my throat. "I'll go for a walk."

# Ask Annie

Ask Annie your most complex interpersonal relationship
questions. Go on, we dare you! All letters to Annie are subject
to publication in the Clayton High School *Register.* Names and
e-mail addresses of correspondents guaranteed confidential.

Dear Annie,
But I really love him. And I really need your
help. Do I make the first move? Will that
make me seem like a slut? But if I wait for
him to make the first move, what if some other
girl gets to him first? I don't want to be too
pushy, though, because you always say that's
a turnoff. WHAT DO I DO?????
    More Desperate Than Ever


Dear Desperate,
I DON'T KNOW!!!! I'm still trying to figure
it out myself.
                                    Annie

# Eighteen

*Scott didn't go* very far, I noticed. Just far enough so that no one else could listen to our conversation.

I could still hear the music—although now the chirping of crickets in the grass beneath our feet was louder than the strains of John Mellencamp. I could still see the people gathered around the campfire, but I couldn't make out their features. We were walking, I noticed, toward the little woods near Kwang's barn. The copse with the stream running through it.

It was kind of funny how Scott and I kept ending up in the woods together.

"If society as we know it ended, and I had to rebuild it," Scott said, leaning down and picking a piece of Queen Anne's lace, "I wouldn't let any actors into my new civilization."

I have to admit, I smiled a little at hearing that. In spite of my hammering heart.

"Oh, yeah?" I said. "What about journalists?"

"Oh, I'd let in journalists," Scott said, spinning the Queen Anne's lace around in his fingers. It looked like a tiny parasol. "Because there has to be someone to record what's going on. So the new society doesn't make the same mistakes as the old one."

Even in the distant glow of the fire, I could see the fingers of his free hand go toward the tiny purple cluster of petals in the center of the flower he held.

My mind instantly flashed back to an afternoon at the retreat. Mr. Shea had told us the old wives' tale that if you pull out the purple part of the Queen Anne's lace, you kill it, because the tiny purple flowers are the flower's heart.

So I went, not even thinking about what I was doing or saying, "No, don't, you'll kill it."

Then I put one of my hands over his to stop him. . . .

And the next thing I knew, Scott had dropped the piece of Queen Anne's lace. And his hands were cupping my face. And he was kissing me like he never wanted to stop.

And I was kissing him back.

And I wasn't even imagining it because I couldn't possibly imagine details like Scott's hands smelling of marshmallow and Queen Anne's lace . . . and feeling so rough against my cheeks, even though they were holding me so gently . . .

and the way his lips tasted, sugary at first and then not at all sugary . . . and the way they felt, soft at first and then not at all soft. . . .

And then his hands weren't cupping my face anymore but had gone to my waist and were pulling me toward him until our bodies banged together and were flush with each other, and I could feel his warm skin against mine, and my arms were around his neck, and Luke's corsage was getting crushed against Scott's chest—

—and the pin that held it to my dress dug into my chest.

"Ow," I said and let go of Scott and took a step back.

"What?" Scott's gaze looked unfocused, and some of the hair on the back of his head was sticking up a little from where I'd run my fingers through it. "What's wrong?"

"Nothing," I said. Because nothing *was* wrong. For the first time in my entire life, it seemed, everything was suddenly, fantastically right. "It's just that—"

"I'm sorry," Scott said. Although he didn't actually sound sorry at all. "But I *had* to do it, Jen. Because . . . because I know I'll probably never get another chance."

I'd been unpinning Luke's corsage as he spoke. Now I dropped it. It disappeared into the long dark grass.

"What are you talking about?" I asked, not all that certain I wanted to know.

"I know you said you were just friends," Scott said. He

sounded more upset than a guy who'd just been doing some pretty serious kissing should have. Especially considering the fact that I'd definitely been kissing back. "But . . . well, I mean, I'm not stupid. He's *Luke Striker*, Jen."

"What does . . . *this* . . . have to do with Luke?" I asked, genuinely bewildered . . .

. . . and starting, from the anxious tone of his voice, to feel less like everything was perfect at last and more like there was something *I* should be anxious about, too.

"I'm just saying," Scott said, like he hadn't even heard me. He wasn't looking at me. He was looking back at the campfire. "When I met you again—at the retreat last summer, I mean—I thought you were . . . well, I thought you were really cool. But I couldn't tell whether or not you felt the same way about me. I mean, you were so nice. But you've *always* been nice. To *everybody* . . ."

If he had stabbed me in the heart, it could not have hurt as much. *Nice little Jenny Greenley, everybody's best friend.*

"It was really hard to figure out what was going on with you," Scott went on, speaking fast and low, like he was trying to get it all out before he changed his mind. "If you liked me—I mean, *really* liked me—or just liked me the way you liked everybody else. And then Geri told me you don't really date—"

Oh my God. Geri was so dead.

"—and I just figured, you know, it wasn't meant to be. And Geri, she was really sympathetic and all, and one thing just led to another, and—"

So very, very dead.

"Well, you know."

Oh, did I ever.

"So I decided, Well, that's that. But it was like—" Here Scott, still not looking at me, ran a hand through his hair in a gesture not unlike one of Luke's. "I couldn't ever really get you out of my head. And the more time I spent with you— you know, at lunch and at *Register* meetings—the more I realized *you* were the one I wanted to be with, and that Geri and I . . . we just weren't right for each other."

Okay. I might let her live. Barely.

Scott finally turned back toward me and, looking down at me with eyes that were unreadable in the darkness, said, "But then Luke came along."

"Right," I said, still not understanding what Luke had to do with it. "And?"

"And . . . Well. He's *Luke Striker*, Jen."

*"So?"*

"Don't *so* me, Jen. You're the one who agreed to go to the Spring Fling with him!"

"Yeah. . . ." I said.

And then slowly . . . so slowly . . . it began to dawn on

me. What Scott was trying to say.

Suddenly, so many things that had confused me before made sense. Like the Dairy Queen napkins. The reason Scott had handed me those napkins instead of kissing me hadn't been because he wasn't attracted to me.

Oh, no. It had been because he thought I was in love with Luke Striker.

*He thought I was taken.*

That was what he'd wanted to ask me, that day in his car. I knew it now. That's what his question had been. Was I, or was I not, in love with Luke Striker?

And suddenly it was like, even though it was still dark out—and to tell you the truth, a little chilly in my chiffony dress—the sun had come out.

Seriously. It felt like the sun had come out and was pouring down all over me, warming me.

"I went to the Spring Fling with Luke," I explained, feeling dazzled by the way he was looking down at me . . . like I *mattered*, "because he *asked* me to go with him. Not because I'm in love with him, Scott. In fact, I'm probably the only girl in this entire town who *isn't* in love with him. And never was."

"Is that really true?" Scott reached out and grabbed one of my hands, then held it—not tightly but not exactly like he was going to let go of it anytime soon, either—in both his own. "Then you're okay with him and . . . him and Geri? You don't . . . You were never . . . ?"

"No, of course not." I couldn't help laughing. I felt like I was in a movie. The sun was shining, little birds were tweeting around my head. I thought any second a rainbow might break out, and a show choir would appear singing "Day by Day." "I was never in love with Luke—"

And then—amazing but true—it just kind of slipped out. The truth. As easily as if we'd been talking about books or something.

"—the way I am with you."

There. I'd said it. It was out there, floating around in space. The *L* word.

Just like that.

I was kind of wishing I could snatch it up and stuff it back into my mouth . . .

. . . until Scott's grip on my hand tightened. Now it *definitely* didn't seem like he was going to let go of it anytime soon.

"Did you just say you *love* me?" he asked.

Well, what was I supposed to do? It was done. I'd said it. There was no going back now.

And you know what? Suddenly, I didn't want to.

"Only since, like, the fifth grade," I said. I knew I was babbling, but I didn't care. "*That*'s why I never dated anybody else. I mean, you moved. But then you came back, and I—"

I didn't get to do much talking after that. That's on account of the fact that Scott grabbed me then and pulled me to him.

And started kissing me all over again.

And this time I didn't stop him.

We kissed all the way through the fireworks display. We didn't even notice that there *was* a fireworks display . . .

. . . I guess because we'd been making fireworks of our own.

When we finally came back to the campfire—Scott's arm around my shoulders and mine around his waist—Trina came rushing up, going, "Where *were* you? You missed all the . . . Hey. What . . . ?" Then her eyes got very big. *"Oh."*

I guess she finally noticed Scott's arm around me. Or maybe she noticed the beatific smile on my face. At least, that's what she told me later. That I had looked beatific . . . even with Queen Anne's lace in the clip holding back my hair, instead of the forget-me-nots I'd started out with.

But I guess you would look beatific, too, if the man you had been in love with since the fifth grade had told you that he was in love with you, too.

Scott agrees with Luke and Geri that I should run for student body president next year. He says he'll even provide all the cookies and muffins and stuff for any bake sales Cara and Trina, who are my campaign managers, might want to hold on my behalf.

And while I never turn down any opportunity to sample Scott's cooking, I do think student body president might be aiming a little too low.

I have to say, I'm thinking, a girl with my people skills? Well . . .

Why not the White House?

# Out and About in L.A.
# People are talking about . . .

Luke Striker, seen yesterday on Rodeo Drive, strolling with current steady, UCLA freshman Geri Lynn Packard, and sporting a bandage on his right bicep. Striker is rumored to be undergoing laser removal for a tattoo left over from last year's tryst with *Lancelot and Guenevere* co-star Angelique Tremaine. . . . .

# NOW PLAYING . . .

See Luke Striker in US 30. . . . Can a high school senior save his Indiana town from a terrorist attack, while winning the heart of the girl of his dreams? Ebert and Roeper call Striker's performance a "tour de force" and give the film "two enthusiastic thumbs-up."

Also starring Lindsay Lohan as "Jenny Green."

# Ask Annie

Ask Annie your most complex interpersonal relationship
questions. Go on, we dare you! All letters to Annie are subject
to publication in the Clayton High School *Register*. Names and
e-mail addresses of correspondents guaranteed confidential.

Dear Annie,
Okay. So I took your advice, and I told him.
And guess what? It turns out he loves me,
too!
   So . . . what do we do now?
   Desperate NoMore

Dear Desperate NoMore,
You live happily ever after.

                                        Annie